TAME ME

TAME ME

MASQUERADE CLUB
BOOK THREE

LILITH DARVILLE

eBook ISBN: 978-1-998127-06-1
Paperback ISBN: 978-1-998127-07-8
Hardcover ISBN: 978-1-998127-08-5
Audiobook ISBN: 978-1-998127-09-2

Cover Design by Atra Luna Design (www.atraluna.de)
Editing by Maggie Morris, The Indie Editor (www.indieeditor.ca)
Formatting by Kate Tilton's Author Services, LLC (www.katetilton.com)

With my Neo
My treasure ... My precious!

You slipped away but kept your promise to let me know you're out there. Our love remains eternal!

CONNOR

Life has a way of fooling us into thinking something good is just around the corner. It's like in those feel-good movies Kat loves to watch. You know the ones—where girl meets boy, they fall in love, and live happily ever after. Sure, they have a fight and break up, but that's because they need to have great make-up sex thrown into the mix. Of course, there are all those movies that show the shiny side of living, the bowl of cherries. Like Forrest Gump, who compares life to all the interesting choices in a box of chocolates.

That's the mood I was in as I cruised around the kitchen making dinner for my Kat, who was due back any moment from taking her ex, Tim, to the airport. I'd been on an emergency conference call with Magnum's US Real Estate Division when Kat sashayed into my office pointing wildly at her watch.

"I'm putting you on hold for a moment. I'll be right back." I pressed the hold button and smiled, trying to hide my impatience. Katherine King, the love of my life, wasn't someone you could ignore when she was on a mission, and she wasn't the type to interrupt without a good reason.

"What's up?" I asked.

"You've forgotten, haven't you?"

I looked at her blankly. "Forgotten?"

She walked behind my chair, put her arms around my neck, and kissed the top of my head. "The airport."

"Oh shit." I had forgotten. I'd agreed to drive Kat's ex-turned-friend, Tim, to the airport while she cooked dinner. We were expecting my best friend, Brian Farrell, and his lovely wife, Asha, for dinner and drinks. It was the first time Kat was formally meeting them, and she wanted everything to be perfect.

"I'm sorry, babe, but I can't leave this call. We could get him a cab."

"I'd rather not. How about I take him, and you start dinner?"

And that's how I found myself buzzing around the kitchen, cooking up a storm, with *Led Zeppelin II* cranked to full volume. Oh, and I should really mention that Kat's the cook in the family, but I make a mean kitchen assistant. That's probably the only place where I'm good at following instructions.

I was well into making the perfect marinade when that box of chocolates with questionable outcome reared its head in the form of the beautiful Asha Farrell.

"Hey, you're early. Grab a seat, and I'll get you a glass of wine."

Before I could make good on my offer, Asha walked over and put her arm around me. "Connor . . ."

I planted a quick kiss on the top of her head. "Good to see you, Ash. Where's Brian? Wait a minute. Let me turn this down." I used the remote to lower the volume on "You Shook Me."

"You'd better sit down," Asha said.

I was so engrossed in my cooking it took me several more

seconds to realize there was something very wrong about her affect. My heart skipped a beat. *Something's happened to Brian!*

"What's up? Is everything okay with Bri?"

"Brian's at the hospital—"

"What?" Panic surged through me, and my heart was kicking the hell out of my rib cage.

"Brian's fine, but there's been an accident. I'm sorry, Connor, but Kat's been hurt."

"That's not possible. She's taken Tim to the airport. She'll be coming through the door any second. There must be some mistake." I'd always prided myself on my ability to face reality, and here I was babbling my denial just like your average Joe.

"Her car went off the road. Tim was pronounced dead at the scene. By the time we arrived, the ambulance was leaving to take Kat to the hospital in Cannes. Brian went with her."

How I had the presence of mind to shut off the stove and remove my apron, I do not know. A part of me detached and orchestrated my actions without my knowledge. Asha hugged me even tighter. I tried to struggle out of her grasp, but she was like a statue holding me in her clutches. It was amazing someone so small could have so much power.

"So she's okay, right? What is it? A broken arm or something? Please tell me she's all right, Asha!"

"She was unconscious, and she was bleeding—"

"Bleeding?" My voice was strident with horror. "From where? How much? For God's sake, talk to me."

"Her head. Brian says she has a head injury and is unconscious. That's all I know. He'll stay with her until we get there."

I ran to the door, grabbing my set of keys to the Cayenne before I remembered that Kat had taken it to drive Tim to the airport. *Shit!* I was about to throw them across the room when Asha took them gently but firmly from my shaking hand.

"I'll drive you to the hospital, Connor."

I sat slumped in the passenger seat of the Mercedes SUV. Despair enveloped me. It was during moments like this that I understood those people who sit in a corner and rock. I could not and *would not* lose my Kat now that I had her back in my life.

The fifteen-minute drive to the hospital in Cannes took an eternity. I stared out the window, frozen with shock, seeing nothing. Asha remained calm and cool as she navigated the late afternoon traffic.

"How did this happen? How were you even there?"

"We were driving in from the airport when we came across the accident. I have no idea how it happened. We recognized your Cayenne and stopped. Brian talked his way onto the ambulance using his Canadian Special Forces creds. He'll make sure she's well taken care of, Connor. You know that."

I slumped further in my seat, unable to move or even think coherently. How the fuck could this have happened?

"Who hit them?"

"What do you mean?"

"I mean, was there another car involved? Kat is a good driver, so someone must have hit them."

"There was no other vehicle. The car went off the road."

"That's not possible. The road from Miramar to Nice is one of the safest roads in the world."

Asha was quiet for a beat.

"We took the scenic mountain route, and I guess Kat had the same idea. There's a gazillion hairpin turns on that route. You know that, Connor."

"Details, I need details."

"It happened on the hairpin loop just out of Spéracèdes."

"Kat is too careful to lose control of the car. That's just not possible."

"Maybe there was a mechanical failure."

"I don't get it, Ash. The Cayenne is new, and we just had it serviced. If this was mechanics, I'll sue the bastards. And what about guard rails?"

"There's a slight curb of raised brick, but it looked like the Cayenne crashed right through it."

"Kat would never be going fast enough to crash through a curb. Was that asshole Tim driving? If he wasn't dead already, I'd kill him."

Asha remained quiet and let me rant. She pulled up in front of the hospital. I jumped out of the car and rushed to the emergency department where Brian stood.

"Here's her husband now," he said. "Connor, this is Dr. Desmarais, the neurologist assigned to Katherine's case. Doctor, Connor McClane."

Husband? That was my cue to follow his lead.

"Where's my wife?" I demanded.

The doctor ran a hand through a shock of jet-black hair. He looked as if he was ready to drop from exhaustion, which didn't boost my confidence one little bit.

"We've taken her down for an MRI, Mr. McClane. We need to ascertain the extent of the head injury she's sustained. It's a great concern that she's still unconscious." The doctor spoke flawless English with only the touch of an accent.

"When will you know something?"

"In many of these cases, it's a wait and see. We should have the results from the preliminary tests in a few hours."

"Tests? What other tests have you done?" I held back my scream of frustration and rubbed the back of my neck. It was everything I could do to keep from leaping down the man's throat. The logical part of my brain reminded me that to him she was just another patient. Every other part of me wanted to shake him into realizing just how important Kat was.

"We've done an EEG, and it shows plenty of brain activity, so that's a good sign. The X-ray doesn't show significant swelling or bleeding, and her skull is intact. The MRI will give us more detailed information about the extent of her injury. After that, we'll run a CT scan, and that will give us a complete picture."

"So, what's the bottom line here?"

Dr. Desmarais sighed. "As of now, all we know is that she suffered a head injury. She may have a concussion, but symptoms are not immediately apparent. We'll know more after she regains consciousness and we assess the damage."

"What kinds of symptoms can we expect to see?" Brian asked.

Common symptoms after a concussive traumatic brain injury are headache, amnesia, and confusion.

"Amnesia?" I asked, hackles raised.

"Amnesia usually involves the loss of memory regarding anything related to the traumatic incident. However, in some cases, the patient will have impaired ability to recall past events and previously familiar information. The memory loss can extend back decades. The good news is the patient usually always remembers who they are, although they may not recognize people who have been significant in their lives. They—"

"Doctor, how about we deal with one thing at a time," Brian said, knowing I was on the brink of losing it. "When will we be able to see Katherine?"

"She should be finished with the testing and admitted in a couple of hours." The doctor looked at his pager as it went off. "You're welcome to wait in the family lounge in the neurology wing. That's where she'll be admitted. I'll look for you there when I know anything else." He turned and hurried off down the hall.

"Fuck! This can't be happening," I said. Fear bubbled through me like lava about to erupt from a volcano. Brian grabbed my elbow and steered me toward the door Asha was entering. She stopped abruptly, turned, and went back out.

"Come on, man. Let's go get something to eat and grab a coffee. Asha will bring the car around."

"I don't feel like eating, and I'm not leaving Kat," I said like the petulant child I wished I could become. That way, I'd have an excuse for the temper tantrum I wanted to throw. I jerked my arm out of his grasp.

"Then don't eat. But we're getting out of here for a bit to clear our heads. There's nothing more we can do at the moment."

"But—"

"We should at least pick up some things Kat will need when she wakes up. You heard what the doctor said. Kat will be having tests for the next couple of hours and pacing up and down the halls isn't going to help. I gave the nurses my cell number, so they can reach us if anything happens."

When we got back to the villa, Brian and Asha insisted I eat something, so I choked down some soup and several quarts of coffee while they each ate something more substantial. I remained in a daze, tormenting myself with a thousand what-if scenarios. One prevailed—what if my Alley Kat died?

After what could have been two minutes or two hours, Asha trundled me off to the car, suitcase in tow. As she pulled out of the drive, it dawned on me that Brian wasn't with us.

"Isn't Bri coming?"

"He's going to check out the Cayenne. He made a couple of calls, and one of his contacts got him access."

I grunted and lay my head back on the headrest. Brian

knew his cars, and if anyone could find out what had happened, it was him. There was no one I trusted more.

We checked in at the nurses' station on the neurology ward. A nurse led us to Kat's room, advising that Kat remained unconscious. And there she lay, her tiny form dwarfed by the bed, a single IV trailing from her left arm. A mass of tangled black curls framed her still face. *She needs you.* As my heart tore, the mantle of calm control finally dropped over me. I would not allow myself to wallow in any more pain. I would do whatever it took to bring Kat through this. I brushed a stray curl and ran my fingers down her arm. Her hand seemed so small in mine, reminding me that she needed me strong.

"I don't care what it takes, I want the best neurologist in the world, and I want him here now."

"I'm on it," Asha said. She knew better than to argue with me.

I sat with Kat and began my vigil.

"I'm here, Kat. I don't know if you can hear me, but know that I love you and I'm not going anywhere." I stared at her, numb and silent, as a lone tear ran down my face.

2

KATHERINE

A weird shade of puce and the smell of chemically altered air assaulted me as I fought my way out of the abyss. *Yes, yes, I'm a bit of a drama queen, and yes, I have my own way of looking at things.*

I think.

At that moment, I was having trouble remembering most things, like how I got there. I cautiously wriggled my fingers and toes and took stock. With the exception of my aching head, all seemed intact.

I was pretty sure my name was Katherine, but even that was a little hazy. There I was, lying in a hospital bed, hooked up to an IV. Oh, and by the way, who the hell paints a hospital room the color of blood? Just sayin'.

What I did know was that an absolutely gorgeous man slept beside me. His head was on the bed, and a set of beautifully tapered fingers rested on my arm. I sensed I knew what it felt like to brush my fingers through the fine brown hair covering his forearm. Even more, I wanted to run my fingers through the brown curls.

Now even I was skeptical about me having thoughts like

this when I woke up in a hospital bed, clad only in their amazingly unfashionable hospital gown, but I had a vague recollection that only unconsciousness kept me from thinking about sex.

Anyway, back to the gorgeous hunk of testosterone sleeping beside me. As I said, I had no idea who he was, but I itched to touch him. The desire to wrap myself in his arms superseded the damned pounding in my head.

Seriously, just look at this guy!

He opened his eyes, and the most amazing pair of gray-greens looked directly at me, startled. He leaped up, obviously agitated.

Calm down, sweetheart. I'm not dying, after all!

"Kat, you're awake. Hallelujah. Are you okay? I'd better call someone."

Hallelujah? Is he the religious sort?

"First, tell me who you are, and then help me get up. I need to pee," I said.

He slowly sat back down, a frown on that beautiful face.

"You don't know who I am?"

"*Nooooo.*" I dragged out the word, striving for patience. Would I have asked if I knew who he was? *Please don't tell me this hunk of heaven is an idiot. That would simply be too much to bear.*

"Do you know who you are?"

Oh God, he really is a simpleton.

"*Yessssss.*" I needed to move things along a little quicker. I really needed to pee. "I'm Katherine. And now I'll ask again—who are you?"

"Katherine who?"

He really was starting to annoy me. Being gorgeous only went so far.

"Katherine Aleia King. Born October 26, 1974.

Address . . ." It was my turn to frown. I couldn't remember my address, but I wasn't going to let him know that. "Address, Toronto," I finished triumphantly. Now can I go pee?"

He reached across me, brushing against my breast in the process, and pressed the call button beside me. "The nurse will be here in a—"

And in bustled the frumpiest nurse. "*Oui? Oh, mon Dieu,* you are awake," she said in a very strong French accent.

"I need to pee. *Now!*"

"You have a catheter, so just let go and urinate," the nurse said.

Nurse Frump busied herself taking my pulse and blood pressure before popping a thermometer in my mouth. *So annoying.* How the hell did she expect me to pee with all these people in the room?

"Everything is good. I must get the doctor."

Thankfully, she left the room. I looked at Mr. Gorgeous pointedly. He smiled.

"I see you haven't lost any of your spunk," he said. "I'm going. Yell when you're done."

"And who am I yelling for?"

"Connor."

Connor? I liked the sound of that. Something about the name felt comforting.

A few minutes later, a flurry of activity announced the entourage that entered the room.

"Mrs. McClane, so good to see you awake. How are you feeling?" asked the man in the white coat wearing the stethoscope around his neck. Nurse Frump stood behind him with Connor a few feet behind them.

Why do doctors ask such stupid questions? I had the good sense not to say that one aloud. And why was he calling me Mrs. McClane? *Am I married to this hunk?*

"I need to conduct an examination. Is it okay if your husband stays in the room?"

Saints be praised. Even though it was a little distressing I couldn't remember him, a thrill ran though me at the thought. The gorgeous man was mine, all mine. And that meant I could jump his bones with impunity. Yay!

The doctor examined me and asked me all manner of questions, some I could answer, most I couldn't. Finally, I got fed up.

"I can't remember, okay? When can I go home?" I didn't know where home was, but I sure as hell didn't want to stay in this place.

The doctor picked up the clipboard at the foot of the bed and scribbled furiously. He handed the clipboard to the nurse, and she left with it. I tried to be patient, but I was really getting pissed off.

"You didn't answer me. When can I go home?"

"We'll have to see, Mrs. McClane. Right now, we need to keep you here under observation. Mr. McClane, can I talk to you outside?"

Connor's frown threw some kind of internal switch. "Look, buddy, if this is about me, anything you have to say to him, you can say to me, right, Connor?" I stared at Connor, and he smiled back at me, and what a smile he had.

"Right." He looked at the doctor. "Anything you'd share with me you can share with her as I'll tell her anyway. I'm sure if she has questions, she'll ask."

The doctor didn't look pleased, but he cleared his throat and continued.

"As you probably recall, I mentioned the possibility of retrograde amnesia to you yesterday, and it appears your wife has a fairly severe case of it. Other than that and the concussion, she seems to have survived the accident without further damage. We'll need to keep her overnight for observation."

Why did he insist on talking about me as if I weren't there? *Internal shoulder shrug.* Oh well, if it made him happy, who the hell cared.

"I don't want to stay overnight," I said. "I feel fine and want to go home." I wasn't sure why, but I had an intense dislike of hospitals. Besides, I was starving for a good meal.

"I advise against that," Dr. Desmarais said. "She's had a traumatic brain injury, and the levels of brain chemicals are altered. It usually takes about a week for these levels to stabilize again. The first forty-eight hours are critical—"

"I'm not staying here for a week. I'll sign myself out if I have to."

Connor moved closer to the bed and took my hand.

"Let's take this one day at a time. Don't worry. I'll stay with you."

"Visiting hours are over at nine o'clock." The good doctor's tone left no room for argument.

"That reminds me," Connor said. "I want to make a rather large donation in appreciation of all the exceptional care you've given us. How do I make that happen?"

"That would be the hospital administrator, but I'm not sure she's available."

"Have her drop by."

Dr. Desmarais opened his mouth then shut it again. He obviously was used to giving orders, not getting them.

"Is there anything else we need to know?" Connor asked.

"Um . . ." The doctor cleared his throat, and his gaze slid over me before returning to Connor. "Have you noticed a change in your wife's behavior?"

"No. What kind of change?"

"Symptoms are not always immediately apparent. She may be sensitive to light and noise. You may notice some irritability and personality changes. Oftentimes, we notice the usual filters that control affect are reduced or removed and normal reactions may become childlike."

"What's that supposed to mean?" I demanded. "Can you put that in layperson's terms, please?"

He looked as if I'd just proved his point.

"Has she always been this—um—outspoken?"

Connor barked a laugh. "Oh yes. You haven't seen anything yet."

The doctor cleared his throat again.

"If you notice any changes, let the nurse know immediately. Now, I'll go see if the administrator is available."

"Thank God that's over. If he had talked about me like I wasn't here one more second, I was going to shit hemorrhage all over him."

Connor looked at me and grinned. "He was a little on the arrogant side, I'll give you that. I've called in another neurologist for a second opinion, and she should arrive tomorrow. Meanwhile, I'll stay here with you."

"But he made it sound like you couldn't stay past nine o'clock."

"Oh, don't worry about that. I'll make a sizable donation and get us moved to a private suite. I haven't run into a hospital yet where money doesn't talk."

"Suite? In a hospital?"

"Babe, all hospitals have suites for the rich and famous. They just don't advertise it."

"Are we rich?"

"Yes, we are."

"How rich?"

"Very."

I gave that some thought.

"Do I have money of my own, or is it all yours?" For some

reason, it was very important to me that I be able to walk away should this man prove to be a demon from hell.

"Yes, you have money of your own." He smiled that crooked little devilish smile that set my private parts all atingle. "And I can see you're still the independent little cuss you've always been."

"Isn't it good that some things never change?" *I think . . .*

3

CONNOR

Several cheaply framed Monet knockoffs adorned the peach-colored walls of the hospital suite. Artificial air rustled the brocade draperies, giving the false impression we had access to the world outside. After exercising the kind of control she called obsessive, involving issuing a rather large check and a move to the suite, Kat lay sleeping peacefully in my arms. The hospital administrator was one of those corporate types with a pentagon of hard edges, but she'd been more than happy to take my money. In exchange, she'd given us the suite for the duration of Kat's stay and granted privileges for the neurologist I'd called in. Dr. Hannah Stern, a preeminent neurologist from University Hospital in London, England, had been more than happy to fly over for a consult and a week's vacation in my guest villa. Luckily, I'd caught her as she was preparing a paper on amnesia to present at a conference in Geneva the following month, so Kat's case proved timely.

The move to the suite had been swift and relatively painless. All was well until Kat found out Nurse Frump had been assigned as her personal nurse.

"Just my fucking luck," Kat had said as Nurse Frump buzzed around like an agitated insect unable to find a resting place. As she fussed with Kat's pillow, Kat looked as if she was ready to give her a permanent place to rest.

"How are we feeling, *ma chère?*"

"I don't know about you, but my head hurts, and I need to lose this IV."

Perhaps the head pain made her a little testier than usual, but I couldn't help admiring her strong resolve. She knew what she wanted and set out to get it.

"Maybe tomorrow, *ma chère,*" Nurse Frump said with an air of insincere familiarity.

"I'm intaking fluids, and my kidneys are working. Do I need to get more graphic than that?"

"But—"

"Ask the doctor now," Kat said, then added as an afterthought, "please."

The nurse looked at me as if seeking an ally. I gave a curt nod, and she bustled out of the room.

When she returned, she removed the IV and gave Kat a shot for the pain.

"That should help you sleep, *ma chère.*" She dimmed the lights and gave me a pointed look. "She shouldn't be disturbed."

I winked at her. "Don't worry, nurse. I'll be sitting quietly on the couch as soon as I say goodnight." I stared back at her until she harrumphed and left the room.

I leaned over and pressed my lips to Kat's forehead. I had to forcibly stop myself from crawling into the bed and gathering her in my arms. I wanted to hold her and never let go.

"Good night, my love. I'll be right over there if you need anything."

Kat yawned, and her eyes started to drift shut. She

popped them open and looked at me. "Can't you sleep here with me again?"

The temptation was almost too much to bear, but I needed some distance to get my anxiety under control. It'd been everything I could do to keep it together. And besides, if that hot little body was beside mine again, I wouldn't answer for what would happen next. "You need to rest and heal. I won't leave."

"Promise?" This time her lids stayed shut.

"Promise." I grabbed a blanket and pillow from the closet and settled on the couch. Except for the catnap I'd taken when I'd drifted off during my vigil the night before, I hadn't slept in thirty-six hours. I closed my eyes, willing the whirlwind of my thoughts to still.

I almost lost her. How did this happen? Will the police find anything? What if she'd . . .

Kat's moaning woke me. "No, I will not count. I . . . will . . . not."

My heart leaped, and my feet followed. She fought with the blankets, and tears streamed down her face. I touched her cheek, and she slapped my hand away.

"Don't you touch me, you bastard."

"Kat, wake up. You're dreaming." I shook her shoulder. "Kat."

Her eyelids flew open. She sat up and looked around wildly, arms flailing, panting. "Get away from me, you asshole."

I stepped back as much to keep a tight lid on my own reaction as to give her space. It took a few moments before rational thought replaced the terror in her golden-brown eyes. I pulled a chair closer to the bed, sat down, and took her shaking hand in mine.

"I'm here. Do you need the nurse?"

She smiled through her tears. "God, no."

"Can I get you something?"

"Just sit with me a few minutes, okay?"

I sat, although I didn't have the faintest idea what to do next. Kat rarely cried, and when she did, they were usually tears of frustration about a situation she had no control over.

"Do you want to talk about it?"

"Connor. Oh, my God. He was beating me."

"Who was beating you?" My heart stilled. Was she remembering the beating that asshole David Thompson had laid on her?

"I don't know. He was a fat, blond guy. I think his name was David," she said, confirming my suspicion. "He had me over a desk, and he was beating me with a belt. He kept shouting at me to count." More tears streamed down her face.

I grabbed the box of tissues and handed it to her. I wasn't sure how someone could be efficient and dainty at the same time while blowing, but she managed it.

"Thank you. I'm sorry. I don't mean to be a basket case like this. It just all seemed so real."

"No need to apologize to me. I'm here for you, babe. Maybe it's more than just the dream. It must be scary not being able to remember much."

"Right now, I find it more interesting than scary, actually. I know who I am, and I know how to *do* everything, at least so far. Like I know how to use a computer and can't wait to get my hands on one. I know my work has something to do with editing books." She tightened the grip on my hand. "And I have you. I can't remember much about you, but I feel safe and secure with you. And very loved."

My heart swelled with something I refused to call joy. "Dr. Stern will be here in the morning, and she'll be able to explain everything to us—that is if you're okay with me being here when she consults with you."

Kat laughed a deep belly laugh. "You are a funny guy. I have the feeling you don't usually tiptoe around like this. Don't you usually just do what you want?"

I grinned back. "Usually, but this is an unusual circumstance." I was so relieved the tears had disappeared and she'd left the dream behind, but I should have known better. When Kat had something on her mind, she was like the proverbial dog with a bone.

"C, do I call you that? The dream felt so real. Did that happen? Was I attacked? Why would anyone want to humiliate me like that?

"Yes, you call me C, and I don't know, babe. My mind doesn't work that way." *Shit!* I prayed she wouldn't see through my pathetic effort to sidestep her question. Dr. Desmarais had said it might cause irreparable damage if she was forced to remember something before she was ready. *Shit, shit, shit!* "Why don't we wait and talk with Dr. Stern."

She laughed again. "You know, you are such a chickenshit. You look like you should be in this bed instead of me."

"Maybe. But I'm okay with you wearing the pants in the family as long as I'm the one who gets to take them off."

"Except when it comes to our sex life. That much I do remember."

"You remember our sex life?" I struggled to keep my voice neutral.

"Just that, so far. At least some things. I'm assuming that since I love sex, you do too, so we had a lot of it. I do have a question, though."

Oh, God. Make it an easy one.

"Did I like to be spanked?"

I almost choked. "Isn't that a little out of left field?"

"Not really. That dream makes me feel like if it hadn't been for the fear and humiliation, I might have liked being spanked, so I wondered if we'd ever done it."

"No, we haven't." How did I tell her we'd tried a flogger once? We had just started her sub training, and spanking was more of an advanced lesson.

"Really, how come?"

"Because you weren't ready for it."

"Huh." She was quiet for a beat, and then she gave her version of a wink. "Well, I think I might be ready now."

My cock stirred despite my best efforts to think about a winter swim in Lake Huron. "That's enough of this talk. Let's get you better first, and then we'll see what's next."

"What does better mean? I sure as hell hope we're not going to wait until I get my memory back to have sex." She yawned.

Good Lord. "Let's just take it as it goes. You'd better get some sleep now."

"Would you mind holding me until I fall asleep?"

Her request took me aback. It was unusual for Kat to ask me for affection. She accepted what I had to give, and that worked well for us.

"I don't know if that's a good idea."

"If you don't want to, that's okay. I shouldn't have asked. I know I barely know you, but I feel safe with you. I . . ."

"It's not that, babe. I just don't want to hurt you." *Or get my ass thrown out of this hospital.* I climbed in beside her and pulled her into my arms. Tension hummed through her like wasps in a hive. I stroked her back and murmured against her ear until her breath slowed into a regular rhythm.

"Thank you," she said. "Will you stay with me?"

"I'll never leave you."

"Don't make promises you can't keep, Connor."

My Alley Kat was back. I'd missed the warmth of her body snuggled into mine. It wasn't something I did often, but I liked knowing I could do it when I wanted to. That was probably not as often as she would like, but she never pressured me to give more than I had to give. That was one of the many things I loved about her.

She slung her leg over mine, and her hand brushed my fly. I went hard as a rock. She made a small sigh that sounded like contentment. I drifted into the memory of the last time we'd lain like this together. I remembered the way the black curls danced around her face when I ran my fingers through their silky softness. The intensity of her eyes, gold streaks radiating her excitement. Those small round breasts she was so self-conscious about, that fit so perfectly in my hands, hands that twitched reflexively at the thought of cupping their soft undersides. And those nipples—how I relished the feel of sliding my tongue over their large juicy plumpness. How I loved to hear her moan when I licked and suckled them.

She had a slender, petite body that she likened to that of a boy, although nothing was further from the truth. I loved the swell of her buttocks and would take those over large hips any day. Her smooth, oh-so-smooth skin colored just the way I liked my coffee, with double cream. The baby-bottom softness of the skin on the inside of her thighs, lying open, inviting. The way her long slender fingers felt as they tickled the inside of mine. Long, elegant legs topped a pair of finely formed feet. She had no idea the effect her rare and exotic beauty had on me. Truth be told, I didn't understand her inability to recognize her own beauty, but I was delighted she chose to share it with me.

I sighed. Keeping up this line of thought was only going to bring me a ginormous set of blue balls. Okay, so they don't really exist—painful, but not blue—but we guys like to get all the mileage out of the concept that we can. Anyway, I had more important thoughts to avoid, like the feeling of relief I had every time I thought of where we'd been before the accident. Kat had wanted to take our relationship to the next level, which would require me to make a commitment I couldn't make. If there was a silver lining in every cloud, Kat's amnesia gave me time to hide in those dark clouds I consciously embraced, to avoid the emotional conflict of a past, long removed, but not forgotten.

So why am I so scared?

4

CONNOR

Nurse Frump bustled in at 6:00 a.m., full of those smiles that never reached her eyes. Thankfully, I'd moved to the couch after waking for a pit stop, so we were spared another sermonette on hospital policy.

"Wakey, wakey, *ma chère*. Time for vitals."

Kat groaned, rolled onto her back, and opened one eye a crack. Nurse Frump stuck a thermometer under her tongue. Kat shielded her eyes with her right arm while stretching out the left to receive the blood pressure cuff.

I rose, donned my rumpled shirt, and folded the light blanket I'd used. I needed some fresh air. *And a shower. And clean clothes.* Nurse Frump frowned as I stood on the other side of the bed and touched Kat's arm.

"Looks like this could take a while, babe. Why don't I find us some coffee?"

Kat muttered something that sounded like "Good idea." The thermometer beeped, and she snatched it out of her mouth. "And some croissants and cheese, please. I need protein." She grinned, giving me the distinct impression that didn't mean cheese. The penetrating stare she gave my crotch confirmed it.

I inhaled a lungful of fresh air as I headed south toward one of Kat's favorite cafés, Lux. It was a good thirty-minute walk from the hospital, and I set out at a brisk pace. I needed to stretch my legs and enjoyed the idea of surprising Kat. As she put it, their croissants were divine and their café au lait was to die for. I enjoyed the walk down the Rue d'Antibes before the street woke to the hustle and bustle of the busy weekday. Lux was closed, but a knock on the back door and a few extra euros got me two cafés au lait and a sack full of croissants, fromage blanc, strawberry jam, and a brioche. That should be enough to satisfy Kat for the time being. She loved her food and knew how to eat. The hospital food just wasn't doing it for her.

Kat had showered and changed into jeans and a light sweater by the time I got back, and she was sitting at the small table in the corner. She smiled shyly as I entered the room. I dropped a quick kiss on the top of her head. She smelled marvelous. I couldn't help the bubble of joy that rose through me at her vibrancy. I pushed away that dark voice that murmured in my head. *Nothing lasts forever.*

She embraced the breakfast, consuming her food with gusto. We'd just finished up when Dr. Desmarais entered with a tall woman wearing pants and button-down shirt with a light sweater thrown over her shoulders. She pushed past the good doctor with a wide smile on her face, hand outstretched.

"You must be Connor," she said as she pumped my hand with a firm grasp. "I'm Hannah Stern. It's so good to meet you. And you must be Katherine." Her large hands enveloped Kat's small one between them.

Dr. Desmarais said, "We're very lucky Dr. Stern—"

"Poppycock. I'm the lucky one." She turned her gaze back to Kat. "Do you mind if we chat for a while?"

"Not at all," Kat said. "I love your upper-crust British accent. What are we chatting about, Dr. Stern?"

"Direct and to the point. I like that. First, call me Hannah. No need to stand on ceremony. Before we get started, are you fine with Connor and Serge staying while we chat? I can assure you they'll both be very quiet."

Kat looked over at Dr. Desmarais. "Are you Serge?"

"Yes."

"Nice name. You should use it more often."

Hannah laughed. The good doctor almost choked and sat down in a nearby chair. I moved over to the couch and Hannah settled into the chair opposite Kat.

"So, Kat. I'm a neurologist, and Serge here has been kind enough to let me consult on your case because it might help me with my research."

She gave me a quick glance. I nodded imperceptibly in return, letting her know I understood and approved the game she was playing with the doctor's ego.

"Oh, I love research. I think I do a lot of research, but I'm not sure. What kind of research are you doing?"

"I'm doing research on head injuries causing amnesia. Do you mind answering a load of questions for me?"

Hannah's casual presentation completely disarmed me, and obviously Kat had warmed toward her. She had none of the usual arrogance of a specialist, never mind one who was deemed to be the world's leading authority in neurology.

"So you think you do research. What sort of research?" Hannah asked.

"That's the thing. I'm not sure. I think it has to do with books, though. I know I miss reading."

"Serge tells me you're aware you were in a serious car accident. What do you remember about the accident?"

Kat sat quietly for a few minutes, then said, "I don't really remember the accident, although I have a strong feeling that something bad happened. But I get a headache every time I try to think about it."

"That's because you're trying to force a memory that's not ready to come back yet. Take your time. We have time."

Dr. Desmarais coughed, and I could feel the tension emanating from him. I squelched a chuckle. Hannah's gaze shifted to him.

"I know you've got grand rounds, Serge. I'm okay here for now if you need to leave."

Dr. Desmarais took his cue and left.

"He really is a tight-ass." Kat rolled the bedsheets between her fingers.

"That he is," Hannah agreed. "Now let's get back to what you do remember."

"That's the thing, it's like I don't remember much, and yet I remember a lot. I seem to remember how to do everything. I know that I love reading and golfing. I just don't seem to remember about people."

"That must be terrifying for you." Hannah jotted a notation in her notebook.

"Not really. Dr. Desmarais said it was probably temporary. I'm more analytical than scared about it. It might be different if Connor wasn't here."

"Do you remember Connor?"

Kat gave me a penetrating stare before looking back at Hannah. "Yes and no. I feel safe with him and feel like I know some things about him. I just don't know how we work together. I need to figure out who I am and how I fit in all of this. I really want my computer so I can do some research."

"Maybe I can help. What would you like to know?"

"How long will this amnesia last? What can I expect? When will these headaches go away? Stuff like that."

"Those are all very hard questions to give definitive answers to, Katherine. In my experience, amnesia like yours is usually temporary and can last a few days to a few weeks. When you're around things that are familiar to you, it may start to come back faster. What we do find is that it comes back in stages."

"Will I remember things in a specific order?"

"No, it will be more random. For instance, you may smell something that stimulates a memory from your childhood, which, in turn, might help you remember something from your days in university."

"Why is it doctors never say anything definitive?"

"Because CYA—cover your arse—is our motto. I'm going to give you a similar answer about your headaches. Usually with a concussion, the headaches dissipate over time, but again, that could be days, weeks, or months. The important thing will be for you to rest and let your body heal. Recovery from a head injury is a slow process and getting your memory back is one small step on that journey."

"What else?" Kat asked.

I sat forward. This I really wanted to hear.

"Join us, Connor."

I took a seat at the table. Hannah turned her attention back to Kat.

"Your affect may be more childlike, and you may be inclined to be somewhat more impulsive than you were," Hannah said. "If you loved ice cream before the accident, you may crave it for a while. Connor, don't try to force her memory. That could be dangerous. Make sure she's treated with kindness and gentleness."

"Except when it comes to sex," Kat said. "No need to be gentle there, right doctor?"

"And that's a perfect example of what I'm talking about.

What makes you say that, Katherine? Do you remember something about your sex life?"

"Not really, but I sense we had lots of it, and we enthusiastically embraced it. I love sex."

"Is that true?" Hannah asked me.

"Um, yes," I said. I wasn't at all sure I wanted to see where this discussion was going.

"And he's really good at it," Kat said. Hannah gave me a look of interest. "So how soon can we start having sex again? I think it will help me feel more like myself again."

Hannah laughed. "It might even help you remember. I think you are both in for a few surprises. You can start having sex as soon as you both want, but let's get you out of here first. I'd like to run another MRI . . ."

My mind drifted off as Hannah outlined her plan for the afternoon. Sex, she wanted to have sex. I'd been so wrapped up in the accident and Kat's condition, I hadn't even thought about having sex. Now it felt as if we were rushing things. I didn't know if I was ready for this . . .

I'd just pulled out my cell phone when the door opened and in walked Brian and Asha.

"I was just about to call you."

"Well, here we are," Asha said. "Where's Kat?"

"She's gone off with the specialist for some follow-up tests. By the way, Ash, good find. Hannah Stern is amazing."

"I thought you'd like her," Asha said, taking a seat on the couch.

"So what's up?" Brian asked.

"Just what I was going to ask you. Let's go grab some lunch at this place I know while you fill me in with what's been going on."

We drove down to Lux and each ordered one of their amazing burgers with fries and balsamic-drizzled greens. As usual, Brian started in without fanfare.

"You need to call Brett. He says it's time for you to go public with your position as CEO. There's more chatter about a takeover bid on the office grapevine. They need a leader to let them know the ship is steady and on course."

"That's what I hired Margaret for. That will have to do for now. I'm not leaving Kat, and we're not leaving until she's well. I'll give Brett a call."

Brett Sandvine was my business partner, and he treated me like the son he never had. That suited me just fine as it was good to have a father figure around. My father died when I was a teen, and Brett more than filled the void. He'd helped Brian rescue me from the depths of my despair when my first lover died. What had started out as a fortuitous business arrangement had turned into a mentorship and friendship. He'd long since given me control of the massive business empire we'd built and stayed on as chair of the board.

I'm a very private person and detest any type of intrusion or judgment of my lifestyle. I had long ago decided, given my involvement with my string of Masquerade adult entertainment clubs and the accompanying lifestyle, it was in the best interests of Magnum to keep my position as CEO under wraps. Brett had reluctantly agreed. We'd hired Margaret Scarpetta as president and the face of Magnum International.

I hid my wealth in a vast network of complex corporate identities, making it virtually impossible for anyone to trace its origins. This arrangement had worked well for years, and I'd been content to explore the inner workings of Magnum from the seat of various operational positions in many of our subsidiary offices. Now, the fiasco with my ex–business partner, Cecile DePoulignac, alerted us someone was getting awfully close to uncovering my secret, and that disturbed Brett and Brian. It disturbed me even more. Anything that put me at risk put Kat in danger.

5

KATHERINE

I had an absolute blast with Hannah Stern. She was smart, compassionate, funny, and not the least bit pretentious. She made having those pesky medical tests almost fun. And best of all, she treated me as if I had a functioning brain even if it wasn't firing on all cylinders. We stopped outside my hospital suite.

"That's all for today, Katherine. You've done well. Get some rest, and I'll see you tomorrow."

"When can I go home?"

"I don't see any reason you can't go home today, but that's not my call. Technically, you're Serge's patient. I'm here consulting under his privileges."

"Oh." Tears sprang into my eyes. *Shit!* Was I turning into a crybaby? You'd think I was having massive hormonal fluctuations with the amount of emotion rolling through me.

Hannah lifted my chin with her finger. "Why, when did Serge say you could go home?"

"In a week." I sniffled, desperate for a tissue. "I don't think I can bear it here that long. Hospitals make me think of death, and the food sucks." Although Hannah's expression didn't change, I could almost feel her stifle a laugh.

"Well, it's his call to make, but let me see what I can do. No promises though, agreed?"

"Agreed." But I was almost giddy with happiness.

Hannah strode off down the hall, a woman on a mission.

I pushed into my room and turned around in circles, singing, "I get to go home. I get to go home." I stopped dead on the third rotation. An attractive fortyish woman with black hair and green eyes sat smiling up at me.

"That's good news, Kat," she said. "When?"

"When what?"

"When do you get to go home?"

"Today, I hope. And you are?"

"I'm Asha, Asha Farrell. My husband Brian and I are good friends with you and Connor."

"How long have we been friends?"

"That's a long story. A long time."

"Why don't you give me the short version?"

She smiled at me indulgently. I knew I was behaving like a petulant child, but I couldn't seem to help myself. The thing was, I had absolutely no recall, no sense of her at all. When I'd seen Connor for the first time after the accident, I *felt* as if I knew him. Something deep in my soul responded to him. I had no connection to this woman at all.

Asha studied me as if taking my measure.

"Actually, you and I have never formally met," she said. "Brian and I were just on our way to have dinner with you and Connor when we happened upon the accident." She stood up, embraced me, then held me at arm's length looking me over. "But I sure am happy to meet you now." She took me by the hand and led me to the couch. Something about her drew me in; she had an easy way about her.

"Look," she said. "I can give you all the dirt on Brian and

Connor, but don't tell them I told you. I've been friends with Connor ever since I met him and Brian some twenty years ago. Brian and Connor have been friends since they were boys. I'm Brian's wife, and I absolutely adore the man, probably just as much as you adore Connor."

"So you know all about Connor, then?"

"Yup, I do. What do you want to know?"

"I want to know why he seems to run hot and cold. Why is he so fucking moody? Excuse my French. And speaking of Connor, where is he, anyway?"

"Oh, don't worry about me and French," Asha said. "I don't know the language, but I do have a mouth that could give any trucker a run for his money. Connor and my Brian had a business call to make. They should be here shortly. As for Con's moods, I assume you mean besides the fact that he's a Scorpio and they're always moody. We'll have to make this quick, but I can tell you more later."

I ignored that jab about Scorpios. Maybe she didn't know I was a Scorpio, and I certainly wasn't moody. Why, you probably couldn't find a more even-tempered person than I was. Asha proceeded to tell me about how a woman named Meredith Kincaid's tragic death had broken Connor's heart when he was twenty-one. Losing her hurt him so badly, he swore off love and all that went with it.

"You see, Connor is more vulnerable to hurt than most men. When he gives his heart, he gives it totally and completely. He handed Meredith his heart, and there wasn't anything to protect him from emotional pain that was too much for him to bear. He hasn't loved since, not until you, Kat. And he's scared to death—of his feelings and of losing you. Your accident has really hit him hard. It reminded him of how little control we have over certain things in this world, and Connor is all about control."

"So, if he hasn't loved since, how do you know all this about him?"

"Because I know how he loves me, and more than that I know how he loves Brian. Brian and Connor have a bond that not even I could break, not that I'd ever try. And Connor just realized a few weeks ago that you're the other half that makes his heart whole. But he's like a baby bird, afraid to fly because he might plummet to his death. When you're ready, you're going to have to be the one to give him the shove out of the nest."

"Why me?"

"Because you're a woman, and you're the one he loves. That's why."

Just then, the door swung open, and Connor and a dark-haired, brown-eyed hunk of a man came through. He was the same height as Connor, but that's where the resemblance ended. Where Connor was long and lean, this man was hard and muscular. I wouldn't want to run into him in a dark alley, that's for sure.

"And speak of the devils, here they are now."

"I thought my ears were ringing," the dark-haired man said. "You're sure as hell looking a lot better than the last time I saw you."

"And you must be Brian." I didn't know him, either, but I felt, well, kind of protected by him. I instantly knew he would kill for Connor and, by extension, me.

"Brian Patrick Farrell at your service, Katherine." He walked over and kissed the back of my hand.

"Oh, brother," Connor said, giving Brian a friendly push aside. "Guess who's going home?" He grinned as I leaped up and hugged him. I did my going-home happy dance with him. Okay, truth be told, he stood there like a statue with movable arms while I danced around him, but I didn't care. I was going home. *Wherever home was.*

"I'll go get the car," Brian said. "Meet you out front."

Asha and Connor packed up my things while Nurse Frump harrumphed her way through the discharge papers, repeatedly emphasizing the care I needed to take with the painkillers. Not even her annoying chatter could dampen my mood. I was going home.

We all piled into a Mercedes SUV with Brian at the wheel. Once we were all belted in, Brian navigated out of the entrance, prepared to make a left turn. I sucked in a breath, trying to ward off the adrenaline rush.

"The highway," Connor said in a tone that brooked no argument.

"Traffic will be a nightmare at this time of day," Brian said.

"The highway," Connor repeated. Brian and Asha exchanged a glance, and he switched the turn signal to the right.

"The highway it is," Brian said.

The ride home was awkwardly quiet. Connor sat, jaw clenched, shoulders rigid, his mood putting a damper on small talk. Brian was right, traffic was a nightmare, but I loved the view of the coast so kept my attention on it. I tried not to think of what lay ahead of me. I tried not to think of what lay behind me. There wasn't much else left to think about. *What's for supper?*

Connor's mood lightened as we drove into a pretty little village called Miramar. We drove through quiet tree-lined streets past large estates, many of them surrounded by stone fences. Brian turned into the entrance of one of them, and we wound our way down a secluded drive. The cutest little villa stood perched on the edge of a bluff overlooking the ocean. Okay, it wasn't all that small, but compared to the palatial mansions we'd passed, this wasn't much more than a cottage.

Connor got out, grabbed my bag from the back, and held the door open for me. Brian and Asha stayed put.

"Thanks," Connor said.

"Yeah." Brian gave him a nod.

"Have a good night," Asha said.

"Aren't you coming in?" I asked.

"Not tonight," Connor said. "We'll see them tomorrow." He shut—no, almost slammed—the door, and Brian drove off.

"Could you have been any ruder?"

"Plenty. Now let's get you settled in."

He didn't seem to be in a bad mood, but he certainly wasn't very forthcoming. I had no idea what to do with him, so I meekly followed him up the few stairs and into a wide and airy front hall.

I *oohed* and *aahed* my way through the large eat-in kitchen, living room, den, office, and a couple of guest rooms, each with its own full en suite. Then we entered the master bedroom, and it was gorgeous, simply grand in a masculine way. I didn't even register him saying, "And this is where you can find me if you need me."

For a moment, nothing existed outside that room, and yet I didn't remember a thing about it—except the bed. That sinful bed. I slipped off my shoes and bounced on the left side of the bed, delighted. I just knew it was my side of the bed. The image of lying with him, naked, laughing with him, naked, scampered through my mind. A spark of joy lit, the first I'd felt since the accident. I turned to him, laughing. It took me a beat to realize Connor stared at me, still holding my bag, looking all, well, prickly. I had no other word for it.

"Let me take you to your room."

I was stunned and followed him, speechless. I couldn't think of a thing to say. So many thoughts rushed through my mind. First, I had to figure out whether I was reading his signals correctly—fuck, I had to figure out what his signals were. And I had to do it before the feelings set in. I reached for my rational mind.

"This is your room. I hope you'll be comfortable here."

Why was he being so fucking detached? And why wasn't I sleeping with him? You'd think I'd developed a body odor problem. I resisted the urge to take a sniff.

"Connor, what's wrong with you? Why are you acting like this?"

Classic, my mind hummed. *Lines right out of some B movie.*

He dropped my bag on the bed.

"There's nothing wrong with me, Kat. I'm just giving you the space you need to heal, time to figure out who you are."

"I don't get it. You heard the doctor. There's nothing stopping me from having sex. You heard her."

"This isn't about sex. This is about figuring out who you are. Figuring out who we are together. Things are different right now. You don't know why you're doing what you're doing. I'm not going to take advantage of that. This is the room you've had since we came here."

I heard the plea in his voice, but my temper flared in all her fury.

"So um, we don't sleep together, is that what you're saying? But we're still married, right? We're attracted to each other, right? I don't get it." I turned away from him, and something in my brain told me to shut up, but it worked slower than my mouth.

"And I don't fucking believe that I'm standing here trying to convince someone who doesn't want to be with me." Tears stung my eyes. But a feeling nagged deep inside that he didn't want to be away from me any more than I did. *Then why are you being such a jackass about it?* Well, two could play that game. I scrubbed the tears away with the backs of my hands.

"You know what? You're right, Connor. This is for the

best." I pulled my shoulders back and turned to face him, hoping the smile I forced didn't look too pathetic. "This is a very nice room. I'm sure I'll be fine here. Thanks for everything." *Now get the fuck out.* I hoped he'd leave before I broke down completely.

He hesitated one more instant, then said, "Goodnight, Kat," and quietly let himself out of the room. I resisted the urge to throw something at the closing door.

6

CONNOR

Oh, what a tangled web we weave. Kat was pissed, and I really couldn't blame her. I didn't know how to act around her. I was second-guessing everything I said or did, adding more confusion to an already difficult situation. Yet, what choice did I have? The doctors told me not to force her memories, and anything I said at this point would do just that.

"You have to be patient and give Katherine the time she needs to find her own way," Hannah told me.

Problem was, I was not good at pretending everything was just peachy. I knew it wasn't about me, but I was afraid I might lose her, and I don't think I can live with that. Not again.

We'd slept apart for the few weeks we'd been here because she needed to heal from the beating that bastard David Thompson gave her. Brian had told the hospital we were married so that I had a say in making sure she got the best care. Yet another lie we were not supposed to talk about. How did I get myself out of this mess I was quickly becoming mired in?

I rolled over and stared into the darkness. Kat was just a

few feet away in the next room, hopefully sleeping soundly, unconcerned about the accident. I wanted her. I needed her.

Be patient, Con. Be patient. Not my best virtue.

I hated being out of control. Not being able to touch her drove me crazy. How did I let her know I wanted her, and that I'd like nothing more than to take her in my arms and have her with such abandon nothing else in this world would matter? Why wouldn't I let her know I was plunging deeper and deeper in love with her?

I really could be an asshole sometimes. Earlier, she'd stood in front of me all hot and bothered. Had I told her how very beautiful she was? No. Had I told her I would like nothing better than to take her right there and then? No. Instead, I'd acted like an idiot and pushed her away.

Why hadn't I held her when the hurt flooded into her eyes? I told myself it was to protect Kat. Okay, it was true I wasn't to push things too fast, but there was another reason. I needed her to remember everything we were before the accident. I needed to look into her eyes and see the love we had for each other. I needed more than her beautiful body writhing in sexual abandon beneath me. Sex was always easy for me. Satisfying the desires of a heart that had only recently let love in demanded more.

I lay exhausted. Visions of Kat danced through my head—an impenetrable barrier between me and sleep. My hand drifted down to the thick velvet rope of my cock, a pillar rising off my stomach, roaring its need to have her, a roar heard only in my mind. I succumbed to thoughts of what I wished I'd done to her, with her, this very night. But that wouldn't have been the right thing to do, or so I kept telling myself. And doing the right thing was my modus operandi.

My index finger whisked through the precum of my arousal, spreading it around the ridge of my circumcision. I imagined my tongue dancing around her lips. Kat's lips, so soft, so full, so sensual. The catch of her breath as I pulled back, just a little, teasing, drawing out the tension building between us. She moved her head forward, trying to capture my lips in hers. I let them brush, then moved back, just a hair, teasing hers. I nuzzled her neck. I traced my tongue through the dimple of her neck and circled the firm, taut flesh of her breast before catching her large erect nipple between my teeth. I bit down, just a little, then sucked.

I added saliva to the viscous coating of precum, allowing my fingers to easily slide along the tender underside of my dick, thumb pressing the pulsing vein running down the topside length. I cradled the hard evidence of my hunger for her in the palm of my hand. Long, slow strokes captured the entire length of the shaft, reminding me of how warm and wet it was inside her.

She lay before me, legs spread wide. I inhaled and almost smelled the way her musk blended with her subtle fragrance. My hard cock stood straight in the air, begging for release. I tamed the beast, not ready to let her go just yet. I swirled the pad of my thumb over the tip of my erection and imagined playing with her big, beautiful clit. I loved the way her rosebud stood at attention, eager for my ministrations. Each quiver, each moan, each shudder, sent shock waves of pleasure through my core. I flicked and rubbed and rolled her hardness until she arched and screamed her release.

I was panting with the effort of holding back, but still I needed more. As her imagined heat enfolded me, I arched my hips off the bed, thrusting into my hand, prolonging the pleasure, imagining her moaning, her need to take me deep within. I cupped my balls with my left hand, squeezing and stroking, enhancing the sensation that controlled my every thought. I become lost in the moment. I shoved into my slick hand. Nothing existed except visions of my Alley Kat as the eye of the tornado spiraled toward release. Cum spurted into my hand, seeping between fingers still moving with every rhythmic contraction, desperately trying to prolong the inevitable.

When my breathing returned to normal, I tidied up and slid between the cool cotton sheets. My hand job took the edge off my physical need but left me yearning even more to have Kat here beside me. I drifted into sleep, wishing my hand cupped the warmth of her buttock.

The smell of a hearty breakfast and raucous laughter greeted me as I opened my eyes to the midmorning light. When given the choice, I was a night owl and slept late. For a split second, I forgot the accident and the whole awkward situation with Kat, and life felt normal. I yawned, stretched . . . and remembered. I pulled on a pair of shorts and followed the noise.

The kitchen was a veritable hive of activity. Pots and pans and dishes covered every conceivable surface, no exaggeration. Kat loved to cook and was very good at it, but she sure as hell knew how to make a mess when she did. Usually I tidied while she cooked, keeping the mess under control. Neither of us liked to leave a mess for the housekeeper.

Kat, Asha, Hannah Stern, and my mentor, Brett Sandvine, sat around the large farm-style table, laughing and chowing down while Brian held forth with one of his stories. The remains of a brunch that would rival any breakfast buffet was spread out before them. I ignored the chorus of "Good morning, Connor," and made my way to the coffee maker. A mug, spoon, cream, and sugar were neatly lined up beside it. I padded over and helped myself to a cup.

"Someone didn't get their beauty sleep," Kat said. Her tone held a slight combative edge.

"Don't worry about our Connor," Brett said. "He's not a morning person."

I'd met Brett some twenty-odd years ago when the peach fuzz of adolescence was still a recent memory. I'd carried on a mad, passionate affair and fallen madly in love with his ward, Meredith Kincaid. The first summer I'd spent with her, she'd stolen my virginity. During the second, she'd captured my heart. Her sudden death had ruptured it, and I'd descended into a dark pit of despair, abandoning medical school in favor of sex, drugs, and rock-and-roll women.

When I couldn't sink any lower, Brett said he couldn't just stand around watching me waste my life in self-pity. He had thrown me a lifeline with the offer of becoming his protégé. I suspected Brian had a hand in this, however, we never spoke of it. With Brett's encouragement and prodding, I'd completed an MBA and helped him grow Magnum into the global media corporation it was today. He'd turned the reins over to me with the position of CEO, reluctantly agreeing to remain as chair of the board and figurehead. I, in turn, would retain a low profile avoiding the scrutiny that goes with being the owner of an international business. I'd convinced him we shouldn't take the risk of exposing the company to the taint of scandal that would accompany news of my ownership of the Masquerade clubs.

"Brian and I are going to the Masquerade tonight. Anyone want to come along?" Asha asked.

"Is that the sex club you were telling me about? Oh yes, what fun. Let's all go." Kat's eyes sparkled in anticipation.

"Not a good idea," I said. *Asha and her big mouth.* Kat had no memory of our previous adventure at the Masquerade Club back home, and I worried it was too soon to throw the France location into the mix.

"Kat and I will pass."

"Oh no, Kat and I will not," Kat said. "I'm going, and that's that."

I looked at Hannah Stern, soliciting her support. I didn't get it. She probably thought I was being overprotective.

"I don't see any harm in her going," Hannah said. "Sounds intriguing, actually."

"Would you do me the honor of accompanying me?" Brett asked Hannah.

"I'd love to. Sounds like fun."

Pissed, although I couldn't have articulated why, I took my coffee and strode through the French doors that led to the patio. It was one of those clear, hot, humid days that I loved and Kat avoided like the plague. The heat waves shimmering off the sand gave me the impression I was about to step into another dimension. Only the *caw* of the slender-billed gulls joined with the pig-like *oink* of the greater flamingos reminded me I was still in this universe. That and the party-like atmosphere in my kitchen.

"What's on your mind, son? I haven't seen you like this for a long time."

It took every ounce of control not to start at the sound of Brett's voice. *Son? Oh boy, I'm in for it now.* No matter my age, when Brett had something on his mind, he would make sure I heard him out. For a second, I thought of playing the deliberately obtuse card but discarded the idea. Brett would keep digging until he was satisfied.

"There's a lot going on right now, that's all. We were just finding stable ground after Kat's assault when this car accident happened. Now, I'm dealing with a woman who has no recollection of who she is or who we are for that matter."

"And she wants to jump your bones, and that's making you decidedly uncomfortable."

"How the fuck . . . ?"

I turned the full heat of my gaze onto my mentor, but I

was no match for the master who had taught me.

"Your Kat certainly speaks her mind, although I understand from the good Dr. Stern her normal character traits are amplified by the head injury."

"Yeah, well, she doesn't know what's good for her."

"That may be, but she certainly seems to know what's good for you. Why not live a little, Connor? It's long overdue."

"I'm not willing to do anything that might jeopardize her recovery, that's why."

"According to Hannah, the only thing that could potentially jeopardize Kat's recovery is trying to force her memory. Other than that, she can live normally and do what she's ready to do. This is more about you than it is her. Think about it."

"Is that all?" I couldn't help the terseness in my voice. Brett had a way of cutting to the chase and making me think. At the moment, I wasn't thanking him for it.

"Unfortunately, I'm going to add to your growing list of sorrows. You need to come back home and take the reins at Magnum. If you don't come back now, you could lose it all, Connor. I can only hold off the board for so long."

"Then, so be it. I lose it all. I won't leave Kat like this, Brett."

"Give your head a shake and think about what you're saying. No fancy cars, no condos, but most of all, no power and control. If she loves you, Katherine will be here when you get back. Or bring her with you."

"The doctor says taking her back to where she was attacked could cause her irreparable harm. I won't do anything to jeopardize her recovery. End of discussion." I glossed over the fact that the doctor I was referring to was the overly cautious Desmarais. I hadn't run this by Hannah because I hadn't wanted to hear her answer.

"I know you're not willing to expose Magnum to the backlash, when the news of your involvement in your clubs comes out, but it's time, Connor. We need to let the world know there's strong leadership at the helm, and only you can do that. After all, it's the twenty-first century, and I doubt anyone will care about the seedier side of your sex life as long as your business acumen is still intact."

"I'll think about it."

"And while you're thinking about that, I have something else you should know about." Brian had come up behind us, silently, as usual.

"Oh, and what's that?" *Will it never fucking end?*

"I have a gut feeling this wasn't an accident. I want to have another look at the car before they junk it. The police have written this off as an accident, so I don't expect much help there," Brian said.

"What makes you think that? Is there something more you're not telling me?" I asked.

"Let Brian follow his hunch. I'm sure he'll let us know when he has something concrete to tell us." As usual, Brett stepped in to calm the waters.

"You two go. I'd better stay here with Kat," I said.

"The girls will be fine. They're going to go shopping and meet us at the club later. Hannah will spend the morning with them. It will give her a chance to assess Kat in her normal environment," Brian said.

Brett said, "Excellent. Connor and I will stay here and take care of some business."

"Okay. I'll meet up with you later this afternoon after I check out the car. We can go to the club together," Brian said.

I knew better than to fight Brian's unerring senses. If he thought something was wrong, something most definitely was.

7

KATHERINE

After a grueling morning of mental acuity tests with Hannah —okay, it wasn't that bad, but I do love the dramatic—Asha and I went into Nice to do some shopping. There were so many neat boutiques, and I discovered another thing about myself—I loved to shop, and Asha assured me I had the money to do so. She helped me pick out several outfits and two pairs of shoes for what looked like an already robust collection back at the villa. We sat contentedly at a café, sipping a couple of cafés au lait while I gorged myself on a piece of the most decadent chocolate cake ever.

"So tell me about Connor."

"What would you like to know?"

"Where to begin? I want to know everything."

Asha laughed. "You'll have to be a little more specific than that."

"Okay, how long have you been friends?"

"I guess it's been about twenty-five years now. Brian's known him since they were boys. When I came along, Connor accepted me as part of the package."

"Sounds like he's more Brian's friend than yours."

"He is, absolutely, although I know him better than most. Connor's a very hard person to know. He's intensely private."

"No shit. Why is that, anyway?"

"Why is what? Why is he intensely private?"

"I meant, why is he so hard to get to know, but it amounts to the same thing."

Asha took another sip of her coffee. For a moment, her green eyes focused on some internal mystery. I busied myself with cramming in another couple of mouthfuls of cake to hide my impatience. What was it with these people? They all thought too damned much.

"You know, I don't know," Asha said. "Maybe it's because he's so independent. Brian says he's been like this since they met. Connor's always lived life on his own terms."

"Did he suffer some kind of childhood trauma?" I sat forward in my chair, eager to hear the melodrama.

"I asked the same thing myself, but no, he didn't. His upbringing was rather idyllic. It's a good bloody thing too."

"What makes you say that?"

"Because of the way he reacted to Meredith's death. I don't know if he would have lived through childhood trauma."

"Tell me more about Meredith."

"I think Connor had better be the one to tell you. I'm sure he'll share it with you when he's ready. I should warn you though, it's a topic he's very sensitive about."

"I'm so tired of everyone treating me like I'm living in some kind of bubble. I lost my memory, not my mind."

"I don't think anyone thinks you lost your mind, Katherine. Connor just wants to make sure that nothing interferes with your recovery."

"Well, keeping things from me is making me mad, which causes me stress, which, in turn, I'm sure, hinders my recovery."

"Okay, okay." Asha laughed. "You win. I'll tell you a little, but you need to swear that it's just between us women."

"I swear, I swear." I put my right hand over my heart and raised my left hand in the air. "I solemnly pinky swear that I will not disclose anything that Asha is about to tell me." I lowered my hands. "There, will that do?"

"You do make me laugh, Katherine. Yes, that will do quite nicely."

"Have you always called me Katherine?"

"I haven't always called you anything because we just met, but I think everyone but Connor calls you Katherine."

Except Tim. He called me Katie.

"Who's Tim?" I asked.

Asha choked, spraying coffee all over the table. She grabbed a napkin and coughed into it. I leaped up and patted her back. When the fit subsided, we busied ourselves cleaning up the mess.

"I'm so sorry," she said. "Now where were we? Oh yes, Meredith. She was Connor's first love, and she died tragically on the day he was going to propose. He's never gotten over it."

"Oh my God, that's so sad. How long ago was that?

"A long time ago. He was around twenty-one at the time. You see, even though Connor seems cold and unfeeling, he actually feels emotion more deeply than most of us if he cares. He can't stand to open the door on any hurtful emotions, so he avoids caring about anyone to ensure he won't be hurt. The only exception to that rule is Brian, and now you."

"So how long have we been together, then? I don't feel like it's been twenty-five years."

"No, it hasn't, but that's all I'm going to tell you. Connor says Dr. Stern wants you to remember as much as you can on your own, so you're going to have to find out from her when it's okay for us to tell you more. Now, let's get going. Supper should be ready for us by the time we get back."

"Who's cooking?"

"Probably Connor's chef. I sure hope so because her food is always excellent."

"Connor has a cook? How come I haven't seen her?"

"Connor has a chef, a housekeeper, a groundskeeper, and a chauffeur. They know to keep themselves scarce when Connor's at the villa."

Connor and Brett were gone when we arrived. No doubt off doing some covert operation around all the business stuff they'd been whispering about. I could have told them there was no need to hide things from me because I wasn't even remotely interested in all their wheeling and dealing. Hannah was there when we arrived; however, and I was interested in what she had to say. She was a hoot. Oh sure, she could adopt the tone of formal doctorese all specialists perfected, but her stories were hilarious. And I saw the twinkle in her eyes when she looked at Brett. I did think there was more than a bit of kink in her.

Asha was right. Dinner was superb, and I was stuffed. Hannah regaled us with stories about some of her colleagues and their research. I laughed so hard my sides ached. Of course, the wine with dinner didn't hurt my mood, either. After dessert, Asha excused herself, presumably to go find Brian.

"So, Hannah, how come you don't want anyone to tell me anything about my life?"

"That isn't exactly how I'd put it, Katherine. With amnesiacs, it's important not to force the return of memory. Often there's a psychological reason the patient doesn't remember, perhaps some trauma they lived through. It's important that we wait until you start remembering before we introduce new information."

"Don't you think the car accident is trauma enough?"

"Perhaps, but there's often some other trigger that we need to uncover."

"Is there anything I can say to persuade you differently?"

"As you recover your memory, you'll ask questions, and we'll give you answers. Why do you ask?"

"Because the name Tim popped into my head this afternoon, and when I asked Asha who he was, she choked and changed the subject."

"Do you remember anything else about this Tim?"

"I don't have memories so much as feelings about things. I feel like I was close to this Tim. It's frustrating I can't remember more."

"It's a good sign you remembered his name. That means your memory's trying to break through. Just don't force it. It will come back in its own good time. Now, don't you think we should get ready for our night out? I don't know about you, but I'm pretty excited about visiting the Masquerade Club. I've wanted to go to the one in London for a long time."

"Then why didn't you?"

"Because I didn't know a member who could take me. The Masquerade is a members-only club and very elite. Security is strictly enforced."

"Sounds very cloak-and-dagger."

"From what I've heard, that would be an understatement."

I'd luxuriated in a hot bath and anointed myself with the lotions and perfume I found in my en suite. I wrapped myself in a thick terry bathrobe and channel surfed to pass the time.

Most channels were in French, but I did find a time-travel show with a very hot guy wearing a kilt. When it was over, it was time to get dressed.

I shed the bathrobe and slipped on a pair of black bikini briefs before stepping into the jumpsuit I'd bought with tonight in mind. It reminded me of something I'd seen before, and I was sure it would get Connor's attention. Made of black satin, it was slit front and back from neck to the shirring at the waist. No bra for this babe, although, come to think of it, I hadn't found any bras in the lingerie drawers in the room. A pair of slinky black heels completed the outfit. If Connor didn't notice me tonight, he simply wasn't human.

Similarly decked out in sexy attire, Asha and Hannah waited for me in the living room. I was positively tingling with excitement as we piled into Asha's SUV and headed back toward Cannes. Somewhere in the countryside, we pulled up in front of a giant mansion complete with uniformed valets. I barely had time to gawk at the splendid architecture before Asha led the way through the massive carved wood door one of them held open. Asha pressed her finger on the panel embedded in the wall beside another door inside the vestibule. A red light shone brightly into her eye before blinking off.

"I can't drink you away," she said. They must have been the magic words because the inner door slid open, and we stepped into another world of opulence.

Something about this was very, very familiar.

We stepped into a large foyer resplendent with paneled walls of alternating gold and walnut, a cathedral ceiling crowned with a crystal chandelier, and gold- and black-veined marble flooring. *Déjà vu!* It was as if I'd traveled through time and stepped back into another era. All I needed was a long flowing gown with one of those low-cut bodices and a dainty piece of lace covering lots of cleavage—in my dreams—to fit in. However, I hoped the jumpsuit I wore would have much more impact.

Brian sat at a large desk facing the door we'd come through. While he and Asha locked lips in greeting, I wandered around the space. Behind the desk were two doors. Door number one looked as if it went into a Star Trek transporter. Door number two was another of those ornate carved wooden doors. Three metal boxes and three masks lay on the desk.

"Ladies, leave your valuables here for safekeeping, including your cell phones and any other electronic devices you have. Then put on these masks so Asha can take you to Connor and Brett," Brian said.

"What's that?" I pointed to the transporter thingy. Something about it was niggling at the back of my brain.

"That's a full-body X-ray machine. Normally, all guests are required to take a scan to ensure they're not smuggling in any devices, drugs, or weapons. We guarantee the safety of our patrons." Asha led us through door number two and down a hallway festooned with paintings.

"We?" Hannah asked.

"Brian and I head up security for all Masquerade clubs."

"So how come we're not having a scan?" I asked.

Asha paused before French doors, each pane filled with etched glass.

"Because you're with me, and I'm fairly certain you're not smuggling anything in that little number you're wearing. Why, do you want a scan?" Asha winked at me.

"Not really. I feel like I've already had one, but I can't think where."

"How's your head?" Hannah asked.

"Pretty good. I have a bit of a headache, but it only really hurts when I try to remember. But enough therapy. We're here to party. Let's get this show on the road."

Asha opened the doors to a bar teeming with people in all sorts of skimpy dress. Rock music streamed through the speakers, and the vibration of the bass guitar shot through me, putting my nipples on full alert. The music wasn't loud, just penetrating.

We followed Asha through the dancers to a banquette in a back but prominent corner. Brett rose as we approached, and Connor followed a split second later.

"Look at you." Brett extended a hand to Hannah and looked her up and down. He kissed her on either cheek.

Faire la bise. So continental. I loved it.

Connor typically revealed very little of what he was thinking and said nothing, but I'm pretty sure I saw a gleam of appreciation in his eyes as I slid into the banquette.

A server arrived promptly and took our drink order. After a few minutes of small talk about our day, Brett raised his glass.

"Here's to new adventures and new discoveries."

We all raised our glasses and took a sip of our respective drinks. No glass clinking here.

"So, ladies, what can we offer for your viewing pleasure this evening?" Brett asked.

Oh good. I was finally going to see what a sex club was all about. One thing I did remember about myself was that I was a bit of a sex junkie. I'd spent so much time thinking and dreaming about sex, I'd worried I was a nymphomaniac. Accepting that my strong sex drive wasn't something to hide from had been a struggle, but I'd done it. *I think.* I'd secretly yearned to see the inside of a sex club, and now that dream was a reality. *Woo-hoo!*

Brett led us out of the bar into a dimly lit hallway lined with doors. The thick carpet effectively absorbed all sound, yet the still air absolutely echoed with the beat of sexual energy. A small viewing window stood at eye level. Brett and

Hannah looked through it before standing aside to let me have a peek. Before me sat a blindfolded woman with rope twisted around most of her body. For all appearances, she sat there alone, exposed for all the world to see.

"What's she doing?" I asked. "That hardly looks comfortable."

"Sex isn't always about being comfortable," Connor said.

Oh, that's helpful. Sheesh.

"Actually, most find it comfortable and soothing. Bondage is probably one of the most popular BDSM games. The *B* in BDSM actually stands for bondage. Some subs like the feeling of helplessness and immobility it gives them. Some just like being on display. Her Dom probably likes the art involved as well as the temporary transfer of control and power," Brett said.

"Very artistic," Hannah said. "This style is Shibari, isn't it?"

"Yes," Brett said. "The Japanese style of rope play is very popular, but I'm surprised that you know about it."

"It doesn't look very safe," I said. "I don't think I'd want to be left alone like that."

"She's not alone," Connor said. "That's against club rules. You just can't see her Dom through the window, that's all."

"I think it's fascinating," Hannah said. "In keeping with my profession, I'm particularly interested in the psychological implications."

"Would you like to see more?" Brett asked.

"Love to."

Brett slid a panel over the small window in the door, and the word *occupied* effectively eliminated our view of the rope-trussed woman.

"We'll catch up with you later." Brett opened the heavy door and gestured Hannah inside.

I turned to Connor. "What next?"

"Let's see if there's anything you'd like to see." He cupped the back of my neck and led me farther down the silent hall-way. Several doors had the Occupied sign before we happened on a sight that made my breath hitch.

"Can we watch this?"

"We can if you like."

A small room with a plush love seat and coffee table stood before a floor-to-ceiling window. Three men sat behind the window at an angle allowing us to see all the action. A young blond guy sat, legs spread wide, firmly planted on the cock of a dark-haired, muscular man. Blondie sat facing away from him, his back pressing against his chest. Muscles' hands held Blondie's hips, and he slid him up slowly, exposing a long, swollen length of rope. Muscles rammed Blondie down, burying his cock deep in his ass and nearly dislodging the slim fellow kneeling at his feet sucking Blondie's cock. Blondie threw his head back and moaned. The man drilling his ass grunted and held Blondie down as he tried to push up. I swear the speakers in the viewing room picked up every breath, every sound, including the wet, sucking noises Slim made as he devoured Blondie's rod.

"Oh, my God." My clit throbbed, and wetness saturated my panties. I didn't know why, but there was something very stimulating and primal about watching these guys together. The intensity of their passion was off the charts. "I can't get over how freely they express their desire."

Connor slipped his hand through the slit in my jumpsuit and lightly drew a line down the length of my spine in answer. And my well of pink pleasure flooded with excite-ment and anticipation. Would tonight be the night? *Hope springs eternal.* I turned to look at him, but his attention seemed resolutely fixed on the scene before us.

Now Slim had a hand wrapped around Blondie's balls and sucked greedily. By now, Muscles, red-faced with effort, did everything he could to prolong the moment. He adjusted himself, no doubt to continue the ride, gripped Blondie's hair, and yanked his head back, effectively stilling him. Muscles twisted his head, thrusting his tongue deep in Blondie's mouth, who greedily accepted, shuddering in complete abandon.

I watched, mesmerized, alternating between fascination with the trio before us and hiding my excitement from Connor, mister control. Well, two could play that game.

"Breathe." His breath whispered past my ear, and I was lost. One word from Connor, and I knew I would do anything he asked of me. *Anything!*

I wasn't sure what that said about me, but I was willing to find out. The bigger question was, would he ask?

8

CONNOR

I watched Kat out of the corner of my eye as the scene unfolded before us. Sexual energy radiated from every pore, and I fought to strengthen my resolve to keep my hands off her until she'd fully recovered. Pheromones rose from her smooth skin like pixie dust coating me with her desire. It was hard for me to connect the woman almost bouncing off her seat with someone needing special care—as if she was oblivious to her recent trauma that remained so vivid for me.

Kat leaned forward as the men switched places. The dark muscular man disposed of his condom before lying with his head facing the foot of the lounger. The skinny little guy crawled over him in the sixty-nine position, knees bent and ass thrust high in the air. Both started sucking with gusto while the tall thin man watched, massaging his cock.

"Oh my God, he's huge. He's going to split that little guy wide open. I can't believe he's going to stick that up his ass."

Subtlety had never been one of Kat's strong points, and what little she'd had disappeared into the vortex along with her memory. The scene definitely stimulated her. What did women find so interesting about watching men together? It did nothing for me, but the steam of fragrant desire drifting from my Alley Kat, now *that* was getting to me.

"He'll be fine." *I may not be.* I selfishly wanted to be the center of her obsession. *Be patient, Connor. Be patient.*

It was everything I could do to keep from slipping my hand through the slit in her jumpsuit and stroking her breast. I settled for running my finger down her spine, knowing the light sensation would drive her wild. Was she remembering that night in the Bahamas? She'd used my credit card to buy this jumpsuit as penance, forgiven me my sins, and taken me to the edge of nirvana with her insistence we have the best make-up sex of our lives. *Shit.* My balls drew up tight and firm, begging for attention. That line of thinking wasn't helping my cause one little bit.

The tall guy rolled on a condom followed by a cock ring. Kat damned near erupted with curiosity.

"Oh my God. What the hell is that for?"

"It's a cock ring."

Kat gave me a funny look. "I can see that. Why is he wearing it?"

"To restrict blood flow to his penis, so he can maintain an erection for a longer period of time."

"Have you ever used one?"

"No. I've never found the need for one."

I tried not to sound boastful, but my stamina was something I took great pride in. I'd worked long and hard to master the control that was my forte.

"Can we try one? And can we try one of those prickly condoms like Muscles is wearing?"

I cleared my throat. "Uh, I don't think so."

"Why not? Oh please, C."

She just called me C. Thank God, her memory is coming back.

"What did you just call me?"

"What? Oh, my God."

She leaped up and pressed her nose against the glass as if trying to get through it into the adjoining room. It was evident Kat's focus was firmly fixed on the scene before us where the tall guy was drilling the puny one. For the moment, I was as good as chopped liver. This was becoming much harder than I thought.

"Never mind," I said. I might as well have been talking to myself.

With a few more grunts, groans, and moans, the big guy and the tall guy came, and puny, jerking himself off, followed seconds later. Before I could blink, Kat straddled me and was ravaging my mouth with her tongue. Desire bolted straight through me to the end of my cock, and she wiggled against it, giving me her own private lap dance. Her wetness soaked through my jeans.

It took every ounce of willpower I had to grab her arms, pushing her away to break the lock her lips had on mine. Breathing hard, beautiful eyes streaked with desire, she wiggled that firm ass again. In one swift movement, I stood and set her on her feet.

"Enough," I barked. "This will not happen, Kat."

"Fine." Her features bunched into a group of dark thunderclouds. "Have it your way. Your loss."

And with that, she stomped out the door, her desire streaming behind her. I adjusted my pants, hoping the pressure wouldn't rupture my dick, and followed her to the bar where she melted into the throng on the dance floor.

I grabbed a drink and found a spot where I could watch the little minx as she slithered and slid her way through the dancers. Kat loved to dance. I didn't, so I was used to her doing her thing with the other ladies who had partners who preferred not to dance. She was an exquisite dancer, and I relaxed while I watched her strut her stuff.

Suddenly a very handsome Saudi prince type stood

behind *my* Alley Kat, running his hands down her sides—did I actually see him brush her breasts?—and grinding his crotch into the firm, round globes of her ass. I stiffened with a jolt. Kat was matching him hip roll for hip roll. *Fuck!* This woman drove me to the brink of insanity and back. Never before had I been the jealous type. Never before . . . *Oh hell, that was then; this is now.* I dropped my glass on the bar and surged through the mob. The dancers parted as if escaping a panther on the prowl getting ready to pounce.

The driving power of the bass bottom ended, and the beginning bars of Gloria Estefan's "I'm Not Giving You Up" started. *Thank God, a rumba.* I pulled Kat from the arms of the smooth operator and into a close embrace. She stiffened for a moment then relaxed into the sway of the Latin dance of love. I couldn't have found a more appropriate song if I'd tried.

We became one molded body in perfect perpetual motion. Her groin lightly brushed mine as we danced. She didn't miss a beat as I glided her from Kiki walks, through sliding doors, and then into a big top. It remained a mystery to me how she could so obviously hold the muscle memory of even the most advanced Latin dance steps yet have no memory of what we'd been to each other. An underarm turn with Cuban walk, led to roll-in, swivel, and spiral. As much as she frustrated and infuriated me, it was clear we were made to move together, to be together. Two halves of one whole. God, how I wanted her. I thought of her with legs spread wide, with that look of wonder and lust in the heat of her eyes.

Not yet, Connor. She's not ready yet.

When the song ended, I kept a tight grip on her hand and headed for the door.

"Connor—"

"Not one word, Kat. I'm not in the mood."

She tightened with resistance but allowed me to pull her along. My new Porsche 911 GT3 RS stood waiting by the time we reached the front door.

Not one word passed between us for the entire ride back to the villa. *Why is she so angry? After all, she knows she belongs to me, doesn't she?* I shut my logical brain down as it tried to argue sense into me.

I'd barely pulled up to the villa when she was out of the car and through the front door. I had to run to catch up with her.

"Kat—"

She turned and faced me down.

"You complete and utter asshole. First, you won't touch me. Fuck, for that matter, you won't even come near me like I have leprosy or something. Then, when I try to have a little fun, and God knows after what I've been through, I deserve a little fun, you have the colossal gall to blow off the one guy who was actually paying me some attention. Well, fuck you, Connor."

I grabbed her arm as she strode by me. She froze, stiff as a lightning rod bristling with electricity, bolts of anger shooting from her eyes.

"Don't. Touch. Me."

I kept my grip on her arm.

"We need to talk."

She stomped on my instep.

Fuck that hurts. I let go of her arm. She headed toward the Great Room, presumably heading for more wine. The fuse she'd lit finally reached its destination, and I exploded.

"Katherine, assume the position."

I'd never exposed her to the full force of my dominant nature. There was so much more she had to learn, both about herself and about submission, before she was ready for that.

However, at that precise moment, she'd aggravated my last nerve and I no longer cared.

She took several steps toward the wet bar sitting in the corner of the room.

"Now," I roared.

For a split second, I thought she'd continue to defy me. Then, in one graceful movement, she slid to her knees, legs spread, head bowed in submission.

9

KATHERINE

Sweet Jesus! Assume the position? Even more unbelievable than the way Connor spoke to me was the way I automatically sank to my knees. *Have I done this before?*

Anger and excitement surged through me. How dare he speak to me that way? Yet those words lit every nerve ending in my body like a Christmas tree, and the battle between morality and depravity continued.

Could it be he was going to make love to me, finally? Desire coiled deep in my belly like a serpent waiting to strike. I kept my head bowed and eyes cast down. I didn't even know how I knew this was the thing to do; I just knew it felt right.

Connor went to the bar and poured himself a drink. He circled around me once before settling in the easy chair in front of the large granite fireplace. I could feel his eyes examining me, sizing up his quarry while he decided what to do with her. *Oh boy. I've done it now.* Anticipation continued to bubble up through me like an effervescent drink poured over ice. Clearly, Hannah was right—my rational brain wasn't operating on all cylinders.

"What am I to do with you, Katherine?"

I wisely kept my mouth shut.

"So, what is it that gave you the urge to throw yourself at that man? And that is not a rhetorical question."

Sweet. He's jealous.

"I wouldn't call it throwing myself—"

"Are you really going to quibble with me over semantics? I want the truth."

He started pacing. There was a seriously dangerous undertone to his deceptively mild voice that sent shivers of lust dancing through my core.

Oh boy. I took a deep breath and tried to push away the fluttering, empty feeling in the pit of my stomach.

"I wanted to have some fun, and you weren't interested, or so it seemed."

I stared at my reflection in the polished shoes that planted directly in front of me.

"So, you decided just anyone would do?"

I couldn't resist being just a little bit saucy.

"He wasn't just anyone, Connor. Did you take a good look at him?"

I had to endure several seconds of silence that seemed to stretch to forever. Then . . .

"I. Beg. Your. Pardon?"

Oh boy. I mentally counted to ten while weighing my options.

"Nothing worth repeating."

He resumed his pacing. Kind of like a caged cheetah—all sinew and rippling muscle, balking at the cage of his own making.

He wanted me. I could feel it. Yet the part of him that held back was like an impenetrable wall. And I suddenly realized he was giving me the key to find my way back to him.

Things had been weird since the accident, but since I

didn't have many memories to occupy my mind, I was free to watch and absorb. I'd learned a lot about this man of mine, this man I couldn't remember yet I knew had always been a part of me. This man, this incredibly sexy, moody, controlling, charming man baffled me. This man they told me was my husband, but who didn't act like a husband, who didn't feel like a husband. *Whatever a husband feels like.*

But then what did he feel like? Oh, in some ways he acted as if we'd been lovers, but he sure as hell wasn't jumping my bones now. They always tell you if a guy's interested, he'll jump your bones. Lucky, lucky me. I get the one man on earth who doesn't fit the status quo. I—oh God, I was getting pissy. That probably wasn't a good thing.

But on a cellular level, I understood this jealousy. Had I been one of those insecure women who think every gorgeous female out there could stop my man's heart with one look? The kind of woman who, when she throws a hissy fit, turns his crank so much he backs her against the door, ramming his thigh between her legs? My momentary empathy vanished, and I started to hyperventilate at the thought of Connor pinning *me* against the door, arms high above my head. Just the thought of the force along with all his hot, smoldering heat had me slick with anticipation.

"Katherine!" His voice was like a whip.

Whoops. Shit. I had no idea what he'd said.

"I think it's time we remind you about submission."

The shards of hot ice in his voice sent a spasm of exquisite torment rushing through my body. *Oh my God.* Was it possible for an iceberg to resist the heat of a volcano? Because the force of both coming from Connor hit me with almost physical force. What was he going to do? Would he spank me? The thought raised bolts of lust and desire and just raw animal need for him. *Get a grip, Kat.*

Abruptly, he stopped pacing.

"Follow me."

I got to my feet somewhat awkwardly and followed him. And then it hit me. *I needed to pee.* Oh boy. It just didn't feel like a good moment to bring it up, not with the vibe radiating off Connor that minute.

He stopped in front of a room, unlocked and opened the door, then gestured me in. I preceded him into the room and caught a brief glimpse of stuff that I associated with having great fun. He pointed to a door on my left.

"I expect you out here in five minutes, naked, and ready to do exactly what I say."

Oh boy.

I did my thing and then removed each piece of clothing slowly, folding each carefully. I hesitated, knowing I was being silly, but I wasn't comfortable with nudity. Oh, I know, I should have been—and I tried to be—but, I wasn't. I'd learned I was the kind of woman who thinks it's okay to call my private parts a cunt, but pussy felt all wrong. Go figure.

Oh yeah, I tried to distract myself with all these thoughts, but my real focus was on the lust cascading through me. *Oh God, I want him.* It was how we might find our way back to each other. I didn't know how else to reach him.

Naked and vulnerable, I went into the playroom. I stood just inside the door, head bowed, while trying to take in my surroundings. Connor stood beside what could only be described as a whipping horse, something black in hand. He'd changed into a beautiful blue robe. Too bad; I wanted him naked. Peeling my gaze from him, I caught sight of a St. Andrew's cross and a display of whips. *Oh boy.*

"So, you think you're ready to play with me, do you, Katherine?"

I figured that was a rhetorical question, so I kept my mouth shut and luxuriated in the calm before the sexual storm that settled over me. This stranger who confronted me in my nakedness was more than familiar. I knew him bone deep. Although his voice no longer held the edge of anger, it commanded nothing short of absolute submission. At that moment, there was nothing I wouldn't do for this man, nothing.

"What are the safe words?"

"Yellow light and red light."

I was having a hard time breathing. Every nerve fiber in my body tingled. One thing I knew for sure—I wanted this. I *needed* this.

"Come."

God, I hope so. My pulse galloped, and I had to take a moment to breathe. I padded over and took the blindfold he held out. White heat washed over me as his gaze inched up my legs and over my belly and breasts, finally landing on my eyes. His mask of passivity did little to hide his desire for me. And his love. Suddenly, I knew with absolute certainty that no other person had received the gift of his devoted passion. It was mine and mine alone. He quirked that damned eyebrow, and I quickly put on the blindfold.

He draped me over the sawhorse, face down, and fastened my wrists in the padded rings attached to the head of the horse. The smooth satin of his robe brushed across my back, sending a wave of pleasure down my spine. Strong hands pushed my thighs apart, spreading me wide for his inspection. Another wave of longing skittered over my skin. I could have sworn I heard a low, feral moan when his fingers swept through the slick juices running down my thighs. I was ready, all right. More than ready.

"Let's see if you remember the rules of engagement."

A snap reminiscent of a strap meeting flesh cut through the air. Goose bumps followed the sound as I squirmed in anticipation. Muscle memory took over, and I relaxed against the bench.

Rules? Oh shit. My heart beat even faster if that was possible. Something stirred deep inside me and niggled at my memory. Tensing, I waited for the head pain. None came. Only the certainty that I needed this.

"Did you want to fuck him?"

Who? I said nothing, enjoying the touch of breeze on my skin as Connor moved, the heat of his hand as it brushed over my left butt cheek.

Crack. The stroke across my ass was sudden and swift. The sting was exquisite, and the embers glowing in my mound burst into flame. The memory hit my body before registering in my mind. *More!* I not only needed it; I craved it.

"When I ask you a question, I expect an answer. Understood?" A delightfully throaty hoarseness infused with lust had kidnapped Connor's usual musical tenor voice.

I shivered and nodded.

Snap. The strap licked the other ass cheek. Desire grew to an inferno raging inside me. My juices ran down my inner thighs, but the echo of a memory blew away embarrassment before it could hit. "God, I love how wet you get." His voice in my mind was reverent with love and lust.

"I can't hear you." The sharp edge in his voice brought me back to the present.

"No."

Slap.

"Pardon?"

"No, I did not."

Crack.

What the fuck does he want? Then suddenly I knew.

"No, sir."

I tasted the word sir, rolling its tart flavor around my tongue like the first sip of fine wine. Tingly and persistent, but the long finish held a note of sweetness to it.

"Did you like grinding your ass into his dick?"

Who knew Connor could be so crude? I loved it.

Snap. The strap caught me high on my thigh. Amazingly enough, it didn't really hurt; rather, the warmth built like a mild sunburn, comforting and welcome. I wanted even more.

"I can't hear you."

"Yes . . . I mean no."

Crack.

"No, sir."

"No? Then why did you do it?"

By this time, the warmth on my ass had turned to white-hot embers nestled deep in my snatch. *And he wants answers while this heat is radiating through my core?* One thought oozed into each tiny crack and crevice of my brain—*Shove that magnificent cock deep and split me wide open.*

Slap. Snap.

Now those stung. I wiggled my ass and welcomed the bite. *Fuck me. Now!*

Crack. That one took my breath away.

"I don't like waiting, Katherine."

Shit. What was . . . ? Oh yeah . . .

"I wanted your attention," I gasped as the building heat hindered my ability to think about anything but what I was feeling between my legs.

Crack.

"Sir."

"You have my attention now. What do you want to do with it?"

The coolness of his touch as he stroked the fire that used to be my ass sent me even deeper into subspace. Every fiber in me yearned.

"I want you to fuck me."

The stroking stopped.

"Sir."

The stroking resumed. The blush blooming in my face no doubt rivaled that fire-engine red of my ass. As crude as my thoughts could be, I didn't much like articulating them.

"All in good time." He continued to rub my ass. "Where are we at, Katherine?"

Huh? I made a half-hearted attempt to get past the wonderful lethargy seizing my mind.

"What light are we at?"

Oh, that. "Green light, sir." *Full speed ahead.*

"Where is my collar?" I had no fucking idea where that came from, but it felt right to say.

"That sass just earned you five more strokes."

Hope springs eternal. Five rapid slicing licks of the strap burned my ass before I'd finished the thought. Tears filled my eyes. My cunt felt as hot as my ass, and I loved it.

A zone settled over me, and my subspace deepened as if I'd arrived home after a very long journey.

"As for your collar, Katherine, you have yet to earn it." He ran his hand through the juice running down my thigh and used it to soothe the inferno that consumed my ass. I wiggled, eager for his hard cock. He chuckled and grabbed both cheeks. I gasped as another exquisite jolt of pain bolted up my tush.

"Not yet, my love. You wanted my attention, and now you have it. But before we go any further, I need to know I, and only I, have your full attention. I need to know you're mine."

I thrust my ass toward him in answer. My God, how I needed to come.

Smack. Smack. Smack. I was breathing hard. Tears started to stream down my face, and still I wanted more.

"Where are we at, Katherine?"

"G–green light."

Slap. Slap.

"S–s–sir."

His hand stroked again. The low and sensual timbre of his voice brought another rush of dew between my legs.

"Who do you belong to?"

"You, sir."

"And when will you grind this sweet ass of yours into another man?"

I said nothing, luxuriating in my tears and the pain of the strokes that followed.

"Now would not be a good time to test my patience. When, Katherine?" That husky timbre deepened even more. His cock would be coming my way very soon.

The coolness of his stroking hand ratcheted the intensity another notch. It was difficult to bring conscious thought past the consuming need to climax.

"Please," I whispered.

"When, Katherine?"

"When you say so, sir."

"Ah, that's my girl. And who do you belong to?"

"You, only you, sir."

Suddenly his hand thrust between my legs, and fingers pinched my engorged clit once, twice, three times. I roared as the orgasm rocketed through me, the strength of the contractions robbing me of breath. As I gulped for air, he grabbed my ass and spread my cheeks. Intensity built as he plunged into me. I had no idea where one orgasm stopped and another began.

I willingly gave myself to this beautiful man. I desperately wanted to be the reason he could no longer keep that iron grip of control on himself, and that he'd let go, fucking me with wild abandon. Just when I thought he'd give up self-restraint, he leaned down and softly whispered, "Let yourself go. Nothing else matters to me but seeing you, feeling you. Show me the exquisite beauty of giving in to your unrestrained desire."

More memories flooded back. Connor's passion was not one of selfish desire. His greatest pleasure was to experience the uninhibited physical expression of a woman losing herself to the moment, and I did. Nothing existed but the blood pounding in my ears and the full ripeness of his gorgeous cock pounding into me. Through me. Taking me. Claiming me as his own. And I came again, and again, and again.

"You're mine." With a great roar, he came.

I shook, almost delirious with sensation as this man, my man, who'd finally claimed me as his own, untied me and gathered me in his arms, rocking me.

"You're perfect." His voice was every bit as reverent as it had been in that shard of memory I'd regained. I curled into his embrace. His semi-hard erection slid over my abdomen, reminding me he controlled himself as much as he controlled me.

In one fluid movement, he lifted me and carried me into the bathroom. He sat me on his thighs, carefully avoiding my aching ass, as he ran a hot bath sprinkled with colloidal oatmeal. He lowered me into it before climbing in behind me and pulling me between his legs. Holding me until the tremors shuddering through me ceased, he washed me, gently cleansing every crevice of my body. When he'd dried me and taken care to thoroughly anoint me with healing lotion, he carried me to his bed.

As he lay me down, I pulled him to me. *My turn!*

Poised above, he looked deeply into my eyes, then lowered his head to pay homage, once again, to my ripe and waiting mouth. In between those air-sucking kisses, he whispered in my ear.

"I want you. My cock strains to fill you. I can't get enough of you."

I placed my hands on his smooth chest, grasping. My

thumbs drew circles around his small, erect nipples. He stayed still as my wandering fingers raked down his flat stomach to the *V* of his groin, round his balls, and back again. Over and over, I used a featherlight touch to a firm hold to make him alter his steady respirations, to no avail. I wrapped my small hands around his cock, mesmerized by the feel of soft skin over hard, polished wood.

Finally impatient, he held my right breast, worshiping it. Licking and nipping with tongue and teeth, he worked me to a frenzy of gasps and moans. My legs parted round him, and I arched to meet him. My fingers dug into his back as I tried to reach him. Maddeningly, his cock, hard and long, brushed against me as he moved out of reach.

Pushing my arms above my head, he went back to work. Slowly, patiently, he took me beyond self-control—the master musician playing his instrument. Alternating between breasts and mouth, he played me until he was ready for the next movement.

"Now, I want to lick you. I want to taste your sweet juices. I want to feel your hard clit as your lips open and you give yourself to me," he whispered as he tongued his way down my stomach to the well of wet between my legs.

He poised, waiting until my thrashing body stilled, arched in anticipation. It took every ounce of self-control I had, but I forced my body to be still. He played my body like a maestro. A major chord rang through me as he fastened his mouth around my sex, tongue playing, moving me to crescendo, and then slowing just before I could climax as he continued the exquisite torture. I went past the ability to give anymore when involuntary spasms ripped through me. And still, he sought more. The intensity of rippling orgasms became too much to bear, and I pushed away from him.

Allowing no respite, he grabbed my thighs and thrust three fingers inside me, manipulating that special spot that pushed me over the precipice of sanity. Exploding in an orgasmic encore, I writhed, screaming with the agony of such pleasure, vaginal walls rhythmically clutching at the source of such joy. The fingers slipped out. He kissed my lips, eyes, and ears, murmuring his vision of my perfection and cherishing me. He hovered above me, his eyes searching mine, seeking confirmation of my complete surrender.

As I arched up to him, the tip of his cock played with the mouth of my open, aching cunt. If I hadn't hated him for it at that moment, I would have admired his consummate ability to control himself. When I tried to coax him in, he moved out of reach, teasing until I slumped toward him panting with disappointment and despair. That's how much I wanted, no, needed his cock to soothe the burning ache deep, deep inside.

The plunge filled me with sensation only previously imagined. Moving together, he took me to heights unexplored, over and over and over again. Conscious thought eluded me as his cock thrust to a rhythmic beat of Connor's making.

The next thing I recalled was lying, gasping for air, soaked with our sweat and combined fluids. Statue still, he held himself above me, watching, filling me with his still rigid cock. As I felt my heart begin to beat again, one thought consumed me . . . I had to taste him, hold him, make him mine. As if of the same mind, we moved in concert, his hands clasping my head as I took his swollen cock in one swallow. Thought no longer existed, only raw animal instinct as my mouth clamped over that lovely appendage.

And still, his breathing remained regular and even. But I'm a determined little cuss, and it was time Connor learned who he was dealing with. This time, control would be mine. Starting with the tip of my tongue, I drew lines up and down the length of his cock, covering every inch before playing with the head, paying particular attention to the soft skin on the underside. Then I went to work with my mouth, playing his cock like a woodwind instrument. Over and over, I worked him, reveling in the feel of that smooth texture brushing the soft inside of my mouth, the head slipping against the back of my throat. I continued like this with the occasional foray into licking and nipping while time stood still. Each time I looked up, eyes smoky with lust gazed steadily into mine, defying my challenge to make him lose control. So, I upped the ante, swallowing him whole over and over; tears ran down my face as I fought my gag reflex. And then, when I'd all but given up hope, his breath caught. With a gasp and a moan, he arched back. Moaning, I clamped down and sucked hard. Connor exploded into my mouth with a keening moan so deep and raw, leaving no doubt how much relinquishing control cost him.

He was mine.

We lay tangled together as the physical subsided to post-coital euphoria. Flashes of similar moments popped in and out of my mind as we lay stroking, our bodies a perfect mold. My sore ass reminded me that he'd claimed me for his own, and I'd willingly given myself to him. I'd liked it. I wanted more.

10

CONNOR

I jolted awake, heart pounding. It took a few seconds to realize what had startled me. Kat lay absolutely rigid in my arms, moaning and sobbing. I could only make out a few words, "Hurting me" and "No, please, no" and "Stop!" Then she arched back and screamed. The terror in that sound scared me to death, more than the sobs and pleas.

Panicked, I shook her. I had no clue what else to do.

"Kat, babe, wake up. You're having a nightmare. Wake up."

She started to thrash around, striking out, and caught me a good one in the gut. *Ouch. Shit!* I grasped her firmly by the shoulders.

"Kat, wake up . . . now."

Her eyes flew open, and she sat bolt upright, breaking my hold, tears streaming down her face. She looked around wildly and continued to strike out. I wrapped my arms around her and held on tight.

"Kat, it's me, Connor. You're okay. You're safe. Come back to me."

I fought to keep the panic out of my voice. Her eyes

continued to dart around the room. Finally, she slumped against me and buried her face in my shoulder.

"That's it, you're okay. You were just having a nightmare. You're okay." Not even sure what I was saying, I continued to reassure her, hoping she'd come back to our reality.

"He hurt me, C. I remember. He hurt me, and I didn't do anything about it. Oh my God, my head hurts."

She grabbed her head and started to rock back and forth. None of this was doing a thing to calm my nerves. Where the fuck was Hannah when we needed her?

"Who hurt you? I'm here now, Kat. No one is going to hurt you." I held her until the sobs died down.

She snuffled. "I need a *Kleenex*."

I reached over and grabbed a handful from the box on the bedside table, handing them over. My heart swelled with even more love as I waited for my strong, brave, and resilient lover to calm. Finally, she blew as if ridding herself of all the pain she'd lived through, then took a deep breath.

She took another deep breath. "My head's about to split open."

I jumped up and brought back a couple of extra-strength ibuprofen along with a glass of water. Kat had remembered something! And just as Hannah had advised, she'd remembered a traumatic experience. I hated that she had to experience so much pain on top of an already painful memory.

"Take these." I waited for her to swallow them before drawing her back to spoon me. "Talk to me. I'm here for you."

"I guess I probably should. I don't think I've thought about it for a very long time. If my head is going to hurt this way every time I remember something, I'd rather not bother. Ignorance can be bliss." She looked up at me with a wry smile that tugged at my heart.

"What makes you think it wasn't just a nightmare?"

"I remember the rape, that's what." She was direct in that way she had of cutting through the noise. *She's too good for you, and she'll leave you again.* I shoved the echo of my deepest fear where it belonged, behind lock and key. Kat needed me.

What rape? Let me get my hands on the bastard. I'll kill him.

Her ex, Tim, had mentioned the rape, but seeing her pain made it real. She'd never talked much about her past.

"I'm sorry. I didn't mean to sound like I doubt you. If you want to talk about it, I'll listen."

"There isn't much to talk about, C. It's one of those typical date-rape stories, sort of. He was at a bar we went to in Toronto. One where they didn't care about ID. Steve was the bouncer and movie star gorgeous. As a mixed-race girl, I was a pariah in the small town where we lived, and I was starved for male attention. He accommodated by plying me with White Russians, free. I had a blast drinking and dancing the night away. At last call, I was so drunk I couldn't move, but Steve convinced me to have one more drink, assuring me he'd drive me home safely.

"When I woke, I was tied spread eagle on a bed. Steve sat beside me." Kat shuddered. "I can still feel the panic that surged through me as he kissed my neck with a knife, threatening to slit my throat if I didn't cooperate."

"The bastard." Not my most articulate, but rage inhibited my usual brain function. I could almost feel the fear emanating from the innocent young Kat. Something had to be done to stop these vermin from preying on the innocent.

"Oh, it gets better. He told me if I screamed, he'd kill me. I had to act like I liked it, or he'd cut me. Everything was blurry. I'd lost my glasses right along with my clothes. I'm sure you can guess what happened next."

I didn't want to know. "Only if you want to tell me."

"Some of the details are fuzzy. I don't know if it was just

the booze or whether he threw a date-rape drug into the mix. Too bad I remember everything he did."

Unlike Brian, I was never one to do violence. In fact, I'd never even thrown a punch except in Aikido practice, but at that moment, I wanted to kill. I couldn't stand feeling the pain that came over me as I imagined how she must have lost hope as that fucker pumped away, knife in hand.

The red pulse beating in my head started to cloud my vision, and I fought not to let this anger overwhelm me. I needed to be there for my Alley Kat. If I was an asshole, I'd lose this chance to get a better idea of why she was such a scrapper.

"He tried to enter me, but I guess it was hard because I was a virgin. He kept trying and trying, and, oh my God it hurt. With each failed attempt, he got angrier. Finally, he rammed the knife handle up my vagina. I started to scream. He said, "Scream, and I'll kill you." So, I bit my lip hard and tried to make my mind go to another place while he did his business. He fucked me. He made me call him Daddy. He made me tell him how good he was... over and over again.

"But here's the thing, I couldn't do it. Detach. My mind simply wouldn't leave the planet. I remember every last fucking awful thing he did to me. When he was done, he untied me, threw my clothes at me, and told me to get out."

I held her, powerless to remove her pain. My own pain almost overwhelmed me, and I couldn't imagine how she'd carried this burden. *You're so strong. How have I ever lived without you?*

"How did you get home?"

"I hitchhiked. By this time, it was three or four in the morning, and the streets were deserted. Some guy picked me up, although at the time I was scared to death he'd rape me too."

"Did you ever see Steve again?"

"Not sure, but I don't think so. But I do remember that knife. He was breaking my hymen when you woke me. I've always hated myself for not fighting harder."

Her belittling herself pissed me right off. "What is the matter with you? Do you have superpowers I'm not aware of so you could have fought back while tied up? If you'd fought harder, he may have killed you."

Kat looked taken aback by my outburst but quickly rallied. "I know. The logical part of my brain tells me that, but the emotional part says I should have fought. Anyway, I know it doesn't make any sense, but I need to submit to turn off the noise and feel my body's responses. I can't really explain it, but when submitting is my choice, that makes it okay."

"Do you remember telling me you needed me to force you?" I held my breath, scared to death that even this small amount of prompting could harm her recovery.

"I feel like I do remember, but that was then, and this is now. I don't want to dwell on the past. I want to get lost in you, become part of you, release myself to you. I want to be your sexual slave."

"Whoa, hold on there. We've only just begun exploring the D/s lifestyle. Let's not get ahead of ourselves."

"Connor, I feel like one thing I've learned about you is that you'll always proceed with caution, usually unnecessary caution." She gave me an impish smile. "And I like to dive right in."

"Oh really, and what else have you learned about me?" I was more than happy to move the conversation in another direction while I got a handle on the churning emotions emerging from her confession.

"Well, let's see. I've learned you pretend to ignore me when you don't want to acknowledge how important I am to you."

Ouch! That hit far too close to home.

"Oh yes, I've learned a lot about you lately. Like how you watch me without seeming to. Like how you hide that hair-trigger temper of yours. I know sex for you is no laughing matter—it's a calling. You know you're the only person I trust with my life, and you sense I want you to dominate me sexually, to push things to our limits."

Too much. Too fast. "Hold on, Kat. If you recall, it was you who was afraid to honestly look at what you wanted."

"I remember feeling shame at the depths of my depravity. That's your word, isn't it? See, I'm remembering." She pumped a small fist in the air while carrying on without a breath. "But for some reason, since the accident, I only feel longing. I long for you to take me. I long for you to make me yours."

"Be careful what you wish for, Alley Kat. This is a dangerous game we're embarking on. I want you to be sure of what you're asking. And we need Hannah's blessing."

She snuggled her butt even deeper against my now semi-erect penis and sighed.

"Not dangerous, C, necessary. And Hannah already gave her sexual blessing. Besides, I want my collar. I've been doing some reading up on it, and if I'm really your sub, you'll give me one. I want to feel that collar around my neck." Seconds later, her breathing slowed, and her body relaxed into sleep.

A sliver of anticipation followed the apprehension slithering up my spine. Oh yes, I'd dallied with giving pain to the subs who requested it. Like anything I did, I'd become an expert at spanking, whipping, rope play, and all manner of punishment techniques, but I'd always approached kink like it was a scientific experiment and never allowed myself to become engaged in the process.

I'd always told myself I wasn't interested on a personal level, and maybe at that time, I wasn't. But now, as I lay here holding the warmth of this woman I loved, who gave herself to me completely and freely, no strings attached, another of the desires I had so purposefully kept submerged surfaced. I held her, stroked her, felt her soft breath across my chest as she rolled in my arms, and finally allowed myself to dream about what I would do with her.

"Wakey, wakey."

The smell of fresh-pressed coffee and the girlish laughter in Kat's voice blew the fog of sleep right out of my head. She was damned near bouncing on the bed with excitement. I cracked an eyelid, then bunched the pillows, rested against the headboard, and took the steaming mug of coffee from her. No point in fighting the inevitable.

"Good morning to you, too." I took a sip of the coffee. Damn, it was good.

"You mean good afternoon, C. You've damned near slept the day away."

"And there's a problem with that?" I gave my usual grumpy response, but in truth, I was very glad to see her enthusiasm for life return.

"Yes, there is. I want you to take me sightseeing. I've been cooped up here too long."

"We were out last night, as I recall. I'd hardly call that being cooped up."

"It's not the same thing, and you know it. Get dressed. Do you want something to eat before we leave?"

"What's the rush?"

"Places to go, things to see. Let's go." She was up and across the room in the blink of an eye. "Oh, and before you even think about it, I've already spoken to Brian, and he says there's nothing you need to take care of, so you're mine for the day."

I bet he did. Bastard. I gave an exaggerated sigh and sat up. In truth, Kat's excitement was contagious, considering the challenge she'd given me last night. Remnants of the old Kat shone through, joining the new Kat, and the devilish twinkle in her eye forewarned me she was about to push my buttons. Well, two could play that game.

"That's your freebie, Kat. I decide when it's a good time to work and when it's a good time to play. Try that again, and you'll get a good hiding."

"Don't make promises you're not prepared to keep, Connor. If last night was any indication, you don't know what a good hiding is." And with that she sashayed out the door.

Damn, she knew how to tempt me.

By the time I'd showered, shaved, and dressed, Kat had pulled my 911 around to the front of the villa. Just the thought of her driving that powerful engine brought back how close I'd come to losing her, and I wrenched open the driver's door.

"I'll drive."

"But—"

"This is not negotiable. I'll drive."

A dangerously stubborn look crossed her face, and she gripped the steering wheel. She was just spoiling for a fight.

"That's one, and if you don't move before I get to two, I'll tan your ass until it's brighter than Rudolph's nose."

A look of speculation replaced the temper.

"That's—"

"Okay, okay. You don't have to get pissy." She got out, casually finding her way to the passenger side, all the while holding that devilish grin.

I adjusted the seat and mirrors. A plan began to form in my mind. So Kat wanted to play, did she?

"Where to?" I asked.

———

We spent a delightful day exploring Turin, Italy. Kat proved to be in one of her far-fetched playful moods pretending she was the reincarnation of Cleopatra as we explored the Museo Egizio, which housed one of the most impressive collections of Egyptian artifacts in the world. Between stops, Kat surfed her tablet, determined to hit every tourist sight.

We took a stroll around Piazza Castello and along the Via Roma before heading to Valentino Park to see the eighteenth-century castle, botanic garden, and medieval village. Caught up in her enthusiasm, and finding her joy infectious despite my usual reticence, I followed her lead. Of course, she insisted on stopping at almost every café we came across.

The afternoon flew into early evening before she announced she was starving. I almost perished while she fussed over restaurant choices before finally settling on the popular Trattoria la Guarnizione, where we tucked in for the next couple of hours, sampling antipasti, pasta, several regional Italian wines, and, in my case, coffee. Kat declared it to be one of the top three meals she'd ever had in her life. *Was more of her memory coming back?* Kat followed dessert with a fine Sicilian wine. She held the stem and swirled the wine in the glass before she gazed at me with shards of expectation in those intense brown eyes.

"Now what, C?"

Our knees touched under the table, and I slipped my hand up her thigh. Just a teaser. She spread her legs.

"We'll have to see, won't we?"

Kat docked her phone, chose her favorite playlist, and sang at the top of her lungs all the way back to the villa. I couldn't stop smiling as I let her melodious tones roll over me while I busied my thoughts with plans for the evening. I wanted everything to be just right as I took the next step in our journey.

The moment we walked through the front door, I put the razor edge of control in my tone, replacing the warm camaraderie of our day.

"Take off your clothes."

"What, here? Now?"

"That's two, Katherine."

"But—"

"That's five. Want to go for ten?"

11

KATHERINE

Right about then I did want to go for ten. Hell, I wanted to go for twenty or thirty. I pushed away the voice in my head telling me it sounded kind of sick, but I was certain that kinky stuff was the only way I knew how to get rid of some of the sexual tension that had built up since I woke from the nightmare.

The few seconds I stared at Connor seemed like hours. He stared back with a glint of steely determination in those gray-green eyes . . . I was about to get a good thrashing. *Make me forget. Make me yours.*

I shed the few items of clothing I was wearing.

"What are the safe words, Katherine?" This time, there was a distinct chill to his voice that sent slivers of electric heat straight to my crotch. Dom Connor might have just come out to play. *Yes, please.*

"Red, but I don't think we need to worry about safe words, Connor. If what I've experienced is any indication, we'll never get there."

My heart hammered in my chest as Connor grabbed my hand and almost dragged me to the bedroom.

"Lie down on the bed." He picked up the flogger lying on the bed.

My ass barely hit the bed when the next verbal lash hit.

"Face down."

He held the contoured handle of a flogger and trailed the lashes across my ass. The tail of long fine rubber strands whispered through the air before striking the soft rise of my exposed buttocks.

For a split second, I wondered if I was some kind of masochist into unbearable pain, but nothing could be further from the truth. Vague memories of spankings reminded me the sting would evolve into little more than a warm ass. What it did do was help me focus on our sex play until I reached that zone where there was nothing else but the pleasure C pulled out of me.

"So, you don't think I can get you to yellow. Well, we'll just have to see about that."

The mildness of his tone might have fooled others, but now I knew for sure. Dom Con had definitely come out to play. Then there was no more time for thought. The flogger bit down in quick succession, and I welcomed the sting of the lashes. As each stroke warmed my ass and thighs, I let go of another of my worries. I quickly became lost in a field of sensation as Connor crisscrossed the strokes over my butt, upper back, and thighs. This time, he wasn't playing, and the bite of each lash built upon the last, fanning a fire that started in my clit and spread through my core until it lit every cell in my body. My endorphins screamed in ecstasy, and I craved every lick of the lash.

With some strange flick of his wrists and my legs, I was on my back, legs apart, the flying tails stroking across my breasts and stomach. It was like watching a maestro in action as the flogger made its smooth arc and landed just where he intended. Then he hit my inner thigh, and what had been the bite of a mosquito turned into the sting of a bee. *Ouch.* Warm heat flooded through me as I welcomed the disconnection from everyday life. As the warmth on my skin turned to fire, I savored the release as I slipped into a zone where thought became the distant buzz of an insect. The only thought in my mind was release.

Another hard stroke landed on the other inner thigh. *Ouch!*

"Yellow," I gasped. I was ready. I needed him.

My man laughed.

"And you said we'd never get to yellow. I hadn't even gotten started." He dropped the flogger and pulled my ass to the edge of the bed. "Do you want me to stop?"

Yes. No. Just make me come. Since I couldn't form a coherent thought, I simply moaned.

"You want me to fuck you?"

"Yes, sir," Right about now, that sounded pretty damned good.

He leaned over me and whispered in my ear, "Not yet, my pet. I'm not finished playing. First, I'm going to lick you. Would you like that?"

Oh yes, pleeease. Frantic with desire, I thrust my hips toward him as his lips surrounded my clit. He sucked it with one long pull. As I moved close to orgasm, he backed off, using his tongue to torture the little girl in her canoe.

He drove his fingers deep into the well of my sex. I surged up, urging them even deeper as he hit that sweet spot of sensation. A waterfall of juices slid down the crack of my ass. Oh, how I needed to come.

"Play with your clit."

His whispered order added to the stimulation, driving me to frenzied heights. I reached between my legs and rubbed the rigid peak that had fully emerged from its protective sheath. He plunged a finger through the slickness coating the pucker of my ass, deep and rough. I exploded, and the blast wave consumed me. I collapsed back on the bed, panting and moaning.

Moments later, the sweet bite of a nipple clamp heightened the waves of contractions pulsing through my core. I sucked air through my teeth as the second clamp hit its mark. Nothing existed but my greed. I needed his cock, and I needed it now.

Keeping my eyes tightly shut, I thrust my hips forward. He pulled the chain holding the nipple clamps. Exquisite pain shot through my distended areolas straight through the juices pumping from between my legs.

"You need to be fucked."

Decisive. Another burst of desire increased the pain in my engorged clit, and babbling nonsense burst from my lips as I begged for release.

The low rumble of his voice was an aphrodisiac all its own. If that magnificent voice was the last thing I heard, I'd have died a very happy woman. He drove into me, the relentless battering ram of my dreams. Over and over, he pounded through the surf of my moist depths until all that existed was the energy I needed to release. I tightened as another climax surged through me. Somewhere in the distance, I heard a roar as Connor's orgasm joined mine, and I surrendered to him.

Eventually, we rose and dressed, but we couldn't seem to keep our hands off each other. I was lost in a fog of sensuality, and I couldn't get enough of this man. Connor seemed to be in a similar frame of mind. He took every opportunity to shower me with tender, loving kisses, to worship my body, and to let me share his love for me.

For once, we were alone in the villa, so I took advantage of having the kitchen all to myself. He came up behind me and circled his arms around my waist, nuzzling my ear as I made us sandwiches in his state-of-the-art kitchen. I'd originally planned on making one of his favorites, croque-monsieur, but decided that was a little too ambitious given my headache and hunger. Since Connor's kitchen always had a plethora of fresh ingredients on hand, I opted for a simple ham and cheese on a baguette topped with lettuce, tomato, and a little butter. Connor, or maybe it was the French, didn't seem big on mayonnaise or mustard as I couldn't find either in the fridge or pantry.

"How's the headache?"

"Still there, but the pills Hannah gave me took the edge off. If it weren't for these headaches, I could almost forget I'd been in a car accident."

"Should I call Hannah? Maybe she can give you something stronger for the pain."

"No, but thank you. She's coming by later this afternoon, so I'll mention it to her then."

"Are you going to tell her about the dream?"

I sighed and ran my fingers through my short curls. "I suppose I'd better since I promised her I'd let her know if my memory was coming back."

I finished making the sandwiches, then turned in his arms and took a few minutes to luxuriate in the feel of those sensuous lips on mine until I was breathless and my toes curled. I unlocked our lips and rested my head on his shoulder.

"You're perfect. I can't get enough of you," he murmured yet again in my ear.

Oh, double fucking ditto, C, and then some. I laughed and gently pushed against his chest.

"I'd better eat something before I faint. I don't know about you, but I'm starving."

He stepped back so suddenly I almost fell forward, grabbed a plate in one hand and my elbow with the other, and led me to the table in the breakfast nook. I looked up into a cloud of concern watching me from those eyes as he placed the sandwich in front of me and pointed to it. "Eat!" I loved watching the myriad of emotions cross his face when he was unaware and hadn't brought them under control. I shivered as postcoital quivers gripped me.

Connor crouched beside me, his gaze lasered over me. "Are you okay? Tell me what you need."

It was lovely to have him fuss over me, and he was so cute when he did.

"I'm fine, C. I just remembered this morning."

The slow, sly smile I gave him did nothing to reduce the worry shining through his eyes.

"You mean the nightmare? I'm concerned that all these memories before you're ready to deal with them will bring about a relapse."

I sighed and pinched my lips together.

"We can't just live in the present. I've got to deal with the past, and I'm tired of everyone trying to protect me from it."

No sooner had the words left my mouth than a massive pain stabbed through my brain while dizziness overwhelmed me. A bloody face with wide blank eyes dropped into my mind. I grabbed my head with both hands and moaned. I wasn't sure which was worse, the pain or those dead eyes. I was vaguely aware of Connor picking me up and carrying me to the couch.

"I'm here, babe. I'm calling Hannah, and I'll be right back."

CONNOR

"Sit down, Con. You're wearing a hole in the floor."

"You're one to talk, Bri. You're just as worried as I am."

Neither one of us could keep still. I kept pacing while Brian twitched and drummed his fingers on the table. I could tell he was dying for a cigarette and refrained only in deference to me. I didn't allow smoking in the house. Oh, it wasn't because of any holier-than-thou attitude I had against smoking, I simply didn't like anything that could bring harm to Kat.

"I'm not worried about Katherine," Brian said. "She's a survivor, and she'll be fine. I've got news, and you're not going to like it."

As intended, that got my attention.

"What kind of news?"

"I asked a buddy of mine at Interpol to look into the car accident for me."

"*Interpol?* Wait a minute. Back up. Last thing I heard, the car was in Cannes."

"Yes, well, while you've been busy with Katherine, I've been following up on a hunch. I called on an old friend from my special ops days. Razor Ramirez is a special forces agent working with Police Services for Interpol, and their headquarters is in Lyon. With his help, I was able to get a look at the car right after the accident. Something just didn't smell right about the whole thing, so I asked Razor to have their forensics department take a close look at it."

"And?" At the moment, patience with a long story was not my forte.

"And, it wasn't an accident, Con. Whoever did it was very clever about it. They modified the computer software so that over a certain speed the car auto-accelerated and the brakes were disabled."

I stared at him in disbelief. *Who would do something like that?*

"I find that hard to believe, Bri. Why would anyone want to hurt Kat?"

Brian gave me a hard look as if I'd just said the stupidest thing known to humankind.

"It wasn't Katherine they were after, Con. It was you."

I was supposed to drive Tim to the airport. But who would target me? "Me? Why would someone over here want to kill me? If we were at home, it might make sense."

"Well, let me see. You run one of the largest and most powerful global media companies where you've no doubt made enemies. You own a string of elite sex clubs where you mix and mingle with the world's richest, some of whom you've pissed right off." Brian held up a finger as he made each point. "Need I say more?"

"Pissing people off is one thing, but I don't believe for a second someone would try to kill me over revoking their membership at Masquerade. Besides, it was Tim and Kat in the car, not me."

"I've been trying to impress this upon you. You think you're invincible, but you're not. And they thought it was going to be you in the car. It was a fluke of bad luck that Kat drove."

I sat down and put my head in my hands as memory came flooding back. That was my fault. I'd been the one who was supposed to drive Tim to the airport while Kat stayed home to cook dinner. I was finally going to introduce her to Brian and Asha. Then I'd received that damned conference call about a takeover bid, and it couldn't wait. So Kat had taken Tim to the airport.

"But they must have had a way to disable the car? Kat wouldn't have gotten anywhere near that hairpin turn if the brakes weren't working when she left."

"That baffled me and Razor, too, and on first pass, they didn't find anything. But you know me—like a dog with a bone. I had them tear the car apart, and they found a very small remote hidden between the gas filter and the fender."

"Yes, but how would they have known where to disable the car? There are no hairpin turns on the coastal highway I usually take, so there wouldn't have been a chance to run the car off the road."

"The remote served as a tracking device so they were able to follow the car at a distance."

I started pacing again. "Who would want to kill me?"

"Use your head, Con. If I can think of someone vindictive enough who wants to be sure your ass is grass, you certainly can."

I stared at him. He sat tapping away with that smirk on his face he gets when he thinks he's got one over on me.

"Prince Nusair Ozer the XIV? I really pissed him off when I threw him out of Masquerade."

Brian barked out a laugh. "No, you're small potatoes where he's concerned. Cecile, you idiot."

"That's a long shot, Bri. I think you've let your dislike of her cloud your judgment."

"Have it your way, Con. One thing that puzzled me was how they'd have known you'd be going to the airport. Think back to that day. Who was here? Did anything unusual happen?"

I started pacing again and cast my mind back to that fateful day. Visions of Kat lying in a coma intermingled with visions of a naked Kat kept dancing before my eyes. *Focus, Connor, goddammit.*

"I can't think of anything. The new housekeeper had arranged for the Cayenne to be detailed, so she'd checked with me to find out if I needed it. I'd let her know about going to the airport."

"You didn't tell me you had a new housekeeper. When did that happen?"

"The property manager arranged it when my assistant let them know I was coming over. Apparently, the usual woman wasn't available."

"*Humph.* Okay, I'll check with her. The mystery deepens."

There was a light knock, and Hannah poked her head around the office door.

"Mind if I come in?" she asked.

"I'll take that as my cue to leave," Brian said. "Hey, Hannah."

"Don't leave on my account," Hannah said.

"We were just finished anyway. See you later."

"So, how's Kat doing?" I gave Hannah a penetrating stare eager to hear about Kat's state of mind.

"She's sleeping at the moment. I gave her a shot for the headache, and she's resting comfortably. Her memory's coming back, and she's going to have some pointed questions for you about the car accident. It's time to tell her about Tim. I would tell her, but I think it's best coming from you, Connor."

Shit. Why me?

"But what about all that pain? That can't be normal."

Symptoms are part of the healing process. All she needs is someone to be there for her.

"I'll never leave her side."

"Now, don't overplay it, Connor. She has to find her own way, too."

I shook my head. The mind boggled. "I need a coffee. Join me?"

"I'd love to."

Hannah followed me into the kitchen where she sat at the island while waiting for me to make a fresh pot. I preferred the taste of brewed coffee over that made in a French press.

"So, when would you suggest I tell her the details of the accident? I don't want to bring on any more nightmares."

"That's probably unavoidable. The nightmares are her way of processing the subconscious images her conscious mind is unable to handle at the moment."

"Is that what's causing the headaches?"

"In part, although the concussion is probably the primary cause. The difficulty here is she's dealing with what in lay terms I call the double whammy—head injury and amnesia. Have you noticed any more changes in her behavior?"

"She seems a little less impulsive than she did a week ago, a little more subdued."

"That could be attributed to some memories returning as she'll be trying to sort out the incoming flashbacks."

"So, what can I do to help?"

It's killing me to see her in this kind of pain.

"It's time you answer her questions, starting with those about the accident, and then be prepared for her response. I expect from what I've learned of her, she'll be quite angry with you for withholding information from her. Don't take it personally and wait it out. She cares deeply for you. She'll get over it."

"So where do we go from here?"

"I've done all I can for her, and she's well on her way to recovering physically. If anything urgent arises, just give me a call or take her to see Serge Desmarais. However, I don't expect there to be a problem in that area. She may benefit from seeing a therapist. I can find out who's good in the area, if you like."

"I appreciate the offer, but I have someone if needed. Thanks for your help. You're welcome to stay for as long as you like."

"I'm due in Geneva day after tomorrow, but I may take a rain check. It's beautiful here, and it's been a well-needed break."

I wrote two numbers on a piece of paper and handed it to her.

"The first number is my pilot's, and you can let him know when you're ready to leave. He'll take you wherever you want to go. The second is for my executive assistant, Stella. You're welcome back here anytime, and if you ever need to contact me, she'll know how to reach me."

I picked up the phone on the first ring.

"McClane."

"Connor, we've got a problem."

Typical of Brett to start a conversation without preamble.

"Which is?"

"Some irregularities appeared in our real estate division. I'm running them down now, but it looks like someone may be perpetrating a fraud here at Magnum."

"What do you mean?"

"I don't have all the details yet, but I wanted to give you a heads-up because I may need you to fly back here to help sort this out."

"I appreciate that. Meanwhile, is there anything I can do from this end? Any leads Brian and I can run down?"

"I'll send a scan of the pertinent documents. See if you can make any sense of where the figures go wrong."

"Done. I'll let you know what we find."

If we find anything. Could this day get any fucking better?

13

KATHERINE

It was late afternoon when I woke. The headache was gone, thank God, but I couldn't get rid of the intrusive memory of those penetrating but lifeless brown eyes staring at me. Whose were they? I wasn't sure I wanted to know but knew I had to. After I changed into a black sleeveless blouse and linen pants and slipped my feet into a pair of sandals, I opened the sliders and stepped onto the balcony, taking in the breathtaking expanse of deep-blue water. A strong breeze washed me in warm sea air. I could never get enough of the strong scent of seaweed and sea salt enhancing the allure of the Mediterranean. The late afternoon sun reflected off the water reminding me that life moves on. There was no denying my hesitation, but I knew it was time for me to move on as well.

I found Connor in his office poring over a stack of papers, his forehead creased in a frown. He wore a fine-knit gray-silk pullover with the sleeves pushed up exposing those magnificent forearms. The urge to run my fingers over those well-formed muscles almost took my breath away.

I ambled over and stood somewhat awkwardly behind his

chair. What I really wanted to do was wrap my arms around him and kiss those delicious lips until his heat drove every other thought from my head. *Want me. Need me.* Instead, he closed the file folder and gave me a brief smile before pushing back from the desk. What I wouldn't give for him to leap up and secure me in the warmth of his embrace. *Always in control. "Loving me will never be easy. Take me for who I am or not at all."* His voice echoed through my mind from somewhere in the past.

He gave me a brief kiss and brushed his hand through my curls.

"Feeling better?"

"Much. But I'm starving. What are we doing about dinner?"

"I haven't given it any thought. What would you like to do? The cook left some confit de canard and the trimmings for us. Or we can go out, if you prefer."

"What the hell is confit de canard? Canard is duck, right?"

"Yes, the French love their duck, and I've acquired a taste for it. Some people think they're in heaven when they eat it with potatoes fried in duck fat. And for dessert, she left a French strawberry pie. What?"

Kat snorts with laughter. "*You* eat duck? This I've got to see. I can feel my arteries hardening already, but sure, I'm game. Do we have any wine to go with it?"

Connor's smile crinkled the corners of his eyes.

"I'm sure we can find something to your liking."

"Then let's eat here, and afterward you can tell me all about the accident."

I watched the smile die from his eyes.

"As you wish."

He turned abruptly and stalked to the kitchen. I followed. I certainly wasn't getting the vibe this was a good time to talk. I set the table while he went to the wine rack and selected a couple of bottles of what looked to be burgundy wine, barely glancing at them. Mental memory told me to relax and wait him out. I took several dishes from the warming oven and peeked at their contents. *Oh my God, this smells—heavenly.* Sure enough, there was duck and potatoes along with asparagus and truffles. A loaf of fresh bread and churned butter finished off the feast. We sat and helped ourselves to the food.

"This looks delicious. Do you always eat like this?"

"Not always." Clipped tone.

Oh great, it was going to be one of those nights. Sometimes getting Connor to talk was like pulling nails out of concrete. Well, two could play that game. We focused on our food and ate in silence. Usually, I was quite comfortable with Connor's silence, but this certainly wasn't one of those moments. His tension sliced right through me. I ate at an even faster pace than usual and practically gulped down a glass of the wonderful burgundy he'd poured. Connor took a few bites and pushed his plate away, getting up to make himself a rum mixed with his beloved *Pepsi.*

"Okay, Connor, it's obvious you're not into small talk, so let's get right down to it. I want to know what happened the day of the accident, every last detail."

Connor sighed, as if the world were coming to an end, and wet his lips. I took another gulp of wine. I wasn't sure I wanted to hear this, but I was determined to face whatever was coming at me.

"You'd better watch how much you drink. It might react with the shot Hannah gave you this morning."

Yes, sir. I managed to bite back the sarcasm, trying not to let his attitude get on my last nerve. You'd think he was the one who'd lost his memory.

"I'll be careful."

Famous last words. I was already beginning to feel the effects of the alcohol. Connor stood and picked up his drink.

"Let's go sit on the terrace."

I dutifully followed him through the villa to the covered terrace facing the heated pool that ran along the length of the house. Connor sat in the only single chair, leaving me the choice of either loveseat or sofa. Why oh, why did this man have to make things so difficult?

"How much do you remember about Tim?" Clipped and to the point.

"Do I know anyone named Tim?" I retorted. I wasn't all that comfortable with this situation, either. After all, it was my life we were talking about here.

"He's your ex, and he was here visiting you. You were taking him to the airport when you had the accident."

And those dead eyes stared back at me. Tim! The image of a handsome face with warm brown eyes laughing down at me replaced those dead eyes. An instant later, it was gone. *Tim?* I gave my head a shake and took another sip of wine.

"He's dead, isn't he?"

I stared at Connor until he met my gaze. Pain clouded his eyes, and I realized this was as difficult for him as it was for me, maybe more so. For a second, I wanted to take away all of the unhappiness that had ever entered his world. But this wasn't about him; it was about me. The thing of it was that I really felt no emotion about this dead Tim. I couldn't remember him. Suddenly, I knew that whoever this Tim had been to me, it was Connor I loved, Connor I'd always loved. It was Connor I could trust and who'd always been there for me.

"So, you're telling me I was married to this Tim before I married you?"

Connor's eyes shifted away from mine.

What aren't you telling me?

"No, you and Tim were never married, but you lived together for twenty years. I don't know all the details. I know only what you've told me."

"So, if we weren't married, and I was with you, what was he doing here?"

"You and he were close friends, and he was concerned about you after you were attacked. He wanted to make sure you were all right."

David. The name flitted through my head and planted itself there. Then, it all came back in a flash . . . along with another headache.

"I remember. David Thompson was my boss, and he beat me and tried to rape me. That's why you brought me here, isn't it?"

I carefully put down the wineglass before pulling my knees under my chin, wrapping my arms around them, and rocking. This was one hell of a lot to absorb.

"Maybe we'd better stop now."

"No!"

Connor's eyebrows rose at the vehemence in my tone. Determination started to settle over his handsome face, so I toned it down a notch.

"Look, I'm sorry. It's just that it's a lot to take in, but I need to know it all. So, I'll be facing this David when we go home? Something to look forward to."

"You don't need to worry about him anymore. He'll never hurt you again." Connor said this in a way that made my blood run cold.

"So let me see if I've got this straight. I got a new job, and my new boss attacked me. You brought me over here, and my ex of twenty years followed. Twenty years. You think I'd remember after twenty years." I was talking more to myself than Connor.

"Something doesn't add up. How long have we been married, then?"

Connor cleared his throat and swirled the ice cubes around in his drink.

"We aren't really married."

"What does that mean, we aren't *really* married?"

"We aren't married, okay?" Connor got up and started pacing. Even in the mood I was in, I couldn't help but admire his feline grace.

"Then why have you been telling me we're married? I don't understand."

Connor sat down and looked like he was in pain as he gazed at me.

"Brian figured the only way the hospital would let me stay with you and give me any information about your care was to tell them we were married. When we found out you had amnesia, the doctors told us not to tell you anything that might push you into remembering before you were ready. So we didn't say anything. I love you, Kat, and we have been together for, um . . . a while. I'm sorry. I didn't mean to hurt you. I did it for your own good."

Famous last words. Shock at the deceit almost choked me.

"A while? How long is a while?"

Connor looked down at the drink still clutched in his hands. "A few months."

"A few months? Oh, this just gets better and better."

It was my turn to start pacing while I worked myself into a fine fury. Connor sat and watched me, which only served to aggravate me further. *Mister Calm, Cool, and Collected.* I stopped behind him and stared down at his bent head.

"You've had plenty of opportunity to tell me the truth since I was discharged, yet you chose not to."

"I just told you, Kat. We were following doctors' orders."

"Fuck, you sound like some cop in a B movie. Don't you

dare put this onto anyone else. You chose this all by yourself. So, under the guise of protecting me, you lied to me?" I was furious.

"I didn't lie, exactly. I just withheld the truth. Would you rather I left you to fend for yourself in the hospital?"

"You will not put me on the defensive here, Connor. A lie of omission—"

"Is still a lie. I know. I know. You've told me many times, and I've said I'm sorry. What else do you want from me?"

The old Katherine would have said, "Nothing." The old Katherine would have let it go. I was quickly finding out that I was no longer that Katherine. I crossed my arms over my chest and glowered.

"What else are you keeping from me?"

"I can't think of anything at the moment, but if there is something else, I'm keeping it from you for your own good." Connor took his turn at being self-righteous.

"You bastard. Of all the colossal gall. What gives you the right to decide just what is for my own good?" I strode around and glared down at him. "You know what I think, Connor? I'm not very happy with you right now, and I'm a little drunk. I'm going to go to bed before I get myself into trouble here. Given your behavior, I'm going to guess you'd rather sleep alone, so I'll be in my room."

I pulled together all the dignity I could muster and stomped off to my room. I needed some time to figure out just why I was so angry and what I was going to do from here. Tomorrow would be a new day. It was time to take back my life.

14

CONNOR

After a few fitful hours of sleep, I gave up trying. I usually sleep soundly, but the state of affairs with Kat left me unsettled. When morning light finally penetrated the room, questions I couldn't answer still besieged me. I pulled on a pair of jeans and went barefoot to the kitchen, determined to put things right. I put together a tray with a pot of her favorite tea, fresh croissants, and a selection of cheeses. I even went that extra step and pulled an orchid from the vase Cook had left on the table. *You're turning into a romantic fool, Con.* Yes, breakfast in bed would be a good start.

I carried the tray up to Kat's bedroom. The door was ajar, so I tapped it open with my foot and set the tray on the small table in the window nook.

"Rise and shine, sunshine." I turned and was greeted by an empty bed. Even worse, it was an empty, made bed. *What the fuck?* Panic shot through me. *You're being silly. She's probably in the bathroom or out for a walk.* Where the hell was she? It wasn't like her to go out without leaving word.

I checked her en suite—nothing. I started a methodical search of the house, and each room netted the same results. I took a deep breath and tried to calm myself. *Think, Con. Where would she have gone?* As irrational as I knew they were, I had visions of Kat in another car accident, lying on the roadside bleeding or, even worse, picked up by some derelict and mugged. *Like that's likely to happen, Connor.* But the catastrophes kept rolling through my mind.

I was dialing Brian and Asha's cottage when he walked through the door.

"Where the fuck have you been?"

"Whoa there, man. What's eating you this morning?"

"Kat's missing. She's gone, and there's no trace of her. I'm not even sure she slept here last night."

"She's not missing. She's visiting Asha, and they're having a girlie chat, which is one of the reasons I'm here so early. And speaking of early, it's not like you to be up this side of noon."

I shook my head and closed my eyes. Of course there'd be a simple explanation for Kat's whereabouts. Bri must have thought I'd lost my mind. *You have, over her. Why don't you just accept it?*

"Don't mind me. Kat and I had words last night. I guess I panicked for a moment."

"Well, we won't hold that against you," Brian said. "I've seen worse. I know what you're like when you get stressed, and what I'm about to tell you isn't going to lower your blood pressure one little bit."

I braced myself for the worst. *What now?*

"Guess who's here in France."

"You know I don't play guessing games, Bri. Spill."

"You certainly know how to take the fun out of a guy's day. Cecile."

I simply stared at him, dazed, while he fought with the know-it-all smile tugging at the corners of his mouth. *Cecile.*

Fuck! Cecile in the same country as me could only mean one thing—big trouble.

Brian moved over to the island and spread several eight by ten glossy prints on the surface.

"Look what we have here."

I sucked in a breath. Staring up at me from the photographs were the unmistakable violet eyes of Cecile DePoulignac, my one-time lover and business partner. Marble-hard beauty did nothing for me anymore, if it ever had. Cecile truly loved only two things, herself and money. She was in equal measures cold, calculating, manipulative, and ruthless. Even worse, she thought she was entitled to own me, and she'd do anything to get rid of any obstacles in her way. Cecile had masterminded David Thompson's attack on Kat, which was when I'd severed ties with her—forever. Beside her stood a large man with his back to the security camera. Something about him jarred a long-ago memory, but I couldn't bring it to mind.

"Who's this?" I pointed at the broad back facing us.

"I'm not sure. Razor and I went through all the security tapes, but we couldn't find a clear one with his face. Are you thinking what I'm thinking?"

"If you're thinking there's something familiar about him, then yes."

"That's what I'm thinking, but I've racked my brain and cannot come up with who he might be. Asha said he vaguely reminded her of someone at the Kincardine club, but the only person we ever met at that club was Ken, and he had flaming-red hair."

"That was over twenty years ago. Besides, there's no way he would know Cecile. No, it has to be someone from a Masquerade club for Cecile to have hooked up with him."

"How are we going to find out what she's up to?"

"Razor and I are on it, Con. I'll have some idea before too long."

"Why would Razor be interested in a couple of random strangers coming into the country?"

"Interpol investigates money laundering and international financial fraud crimes. They also work with international police departments to disrupt and dismantle human trafficking rings. That's how Razor got involved with them. Cecile's travel companion's name triggered an alert when they cleared customs. The name on the passport wasn't familiar and may prove to be phony, but they have to trace it down. They've got a tail on them."

I knew Brian; he had more than this up his sleeve, but I knew it would be useless to question him further. He'd disclose if and when he was ready to. I picked up the ringing phone.

"McClane."

"Connor, this is Stella. Am I catching you at a bad moment?"

It was just like my executive assistant to be considerate of my time no matter how urgent the reason for her call.

"It's always a good moment for you, Stella. What's up?"

"You're not going to like this, Connor."

If I had a buck for every time I'd heard that recently, I'd be an even wealthier man.

"Not going to like what?"

"Cecile called, and she wants to see you."

"Well, you can tell her to go fuck herself."

Normally, I would never be that crude with Stella, but I wanted her to be sure she delivered that exact message to Cecile. Silence was the only response, and I waited a few beats.

"You still there?"

"Yes, I'm still here, Connor. I don't think that's your

wisest course of action. Cecile expected you to say just that, so she said to mention you'd lose everything if you didn't meet with her."

"Fine, then I lose everything."

"That isn't what has me concerned. She asked how Kat was doing after her unfortunate car accident, and I have to tell you, the way she said it sent prickles of ice right up my spine."

It was my turn to say nothing. *She dares to threaten me?* Fury and frustration battled for first place in my battered psyche.

"If that's about Cecile, you need to see her," Brian said.

"I'm going to put you on hold for a moment, Stella."

I put the call on hold and turned my attention to Brian.

"What's she want?" he asked.

"She wants to see me, and she asked how Kat's doing after the unfortunate car accident."

"So, you'll see her. I'll put a tail on her and set up surveillance. Play along, Con."

"I will not. I will not give in to that bitch."

"Okay, have it your way. We'll just sit back and see what she does next."

Shit. Brian sure knew how to get to my jugular.

"All right, all right." I sighed and hit the hold button.

"You there, Stella?"

"Indeed I am. So?"

"So set up a meeting with her in the Nice office tomorrow at nine a.m. Having to get up that early ought to piss off the bitch."

"Consider it done. Do you want me to have them get your suite ready at the hotel?"

"Yes, please. Brian and I will be there a couple of days. Actually, have them hold the suite until further notice. Just in case. Thanks, Stella."

Brian headed for the door.

"I'll send Kat back so you can say goodbye. We'll head out in an hour. I'll drive," he said.

I slipped on a light sweater and a pair of black jeans. The fall days were getting a bit cooler but remained quite pleasant. I quickly packed a bag with a few essentials. I kept a spare suit at the Nice office, and I'd buy anything else if need be. The door slammed, and Kat's sandals tapped across the terrazzo floor.

"I'm in here," I yelled from my bedroom.

Kat walked in with a saucy little swagger of that magnificent tush of hers.

"Brian says you bellowed for me." She took in the overnight bag and the socks, briefs, and T-shirts on the bed.

"I didn't bellow, and I doubt Brian said so," I grumbled.

"Okay, okay. Sheesh. You have absolutely no sense of humor when you're in a mood, do you?"

I refused to get into it with Kat right now. She was in danger, and I had to fix it. Nothing else mattered.

"I've got to go to our Nice office for a couple of days, and I didn't want to leave things the way they are."

"Oh? And how are they, Connor?"

Sometimes I really hated when she messed with me. I sighed.

"Look, Kat, I love you, and you love me. Things have been rough for you, for us, since the accident, but we can work these things out. I know it's bad timing, but I have an emergency I need to take care of at Magnum."

Kat crossed the room and sat on the bed.

"Is everything all right?"

"I'll know better once I've had these meetings. I'm sure it's nothing I can't handle." I slipped into the snug fit of my usual bravado.

"How about I come with you?"

"Not this time."

"Boy, you sure know how to make a woman feel treasured."

And on that note, she flounced out.

Brian and I spent the ride to Nice strategizing. The valet had my room key ready upon arrival. As soon as we hit the suite, Brian called Razor for an update, but he had nothing to report. We ordered room service and debated plans of action well into the night.

I caught a few hours of restless sleep, rose early, and showered. Brian had coffee ready when I emerged from my room. We sat on the balcony overlooking the wide expanse of the Mediterranean and drank in silence.

"Okay, let's get this show on the road," I said.

We walked through the bevy of busy corporate office bees that earmarked any Magnum divisional office. Stella sat waiting at the desk outside my office.

"This is unexpected," I said.

The woman was a saint. She would have flown eleven hours since our chat yesterday. She never disappointed, and I truly admired her dedication. She simply nodded and held the door to my office while Brian and I strode through.

I opened the lone file sitting in the middle of the contemporary wooden desk while Brian checked the paintings and lamps to be sure the cameras and microphones were securely in place.

"There isn't much in here about what Cecile's been doing for the past few months."

"We tracked her to Dubai, and she dropped out of sight. I expect she hooked up with one of the Arab princes she was so fond of playing with at Masquerade. The intel from Razor was the first indication we had that she'd surfaced." Brian crossed to the desk and pressed a code into the phone.

"Are we all set?"

"All set. I'll monitor from the security office."

The intercom buzzed. I activated the speaker. "Yes, Stella?"

"Miss DePoulignac is here to see you."

"Send her in."

Seconds later, the door opened, and my nemesis walked through looking as stunning, cold, and calculating as ever. She glided over to the desk.

"Hello, Connor, darling. Aren't you going to get up and say hello? After all, it's been a long time."

She said this as if I hadn't severed all ties with her and thrown her out of my life. What did it take to get through to her?

She casually looked over at Brian, almost as if he weren't there.

"Oh, I see you kept your stupid little lapdog around for your amusement."

Brian simply smiled and said, "I believe you've cornered the market on the mangy mutt measuring scale."

"Listen, you little bastard, you are just an ant that will soon be on the bottom of my shoe."

"Something to look forward to." Brian quietly closed the door as he left.

"What do you want, Cecile?" Keeping my end goal in mind, I tried to keep my distaste for her from my voice.

She wiggled her hips while she smoothed her hands down the sheath that clung to every one of her perfectly proportioned curves.

"Connor, you really don't want to piss me off any more than you already have." She sat on the leather couch opposite the desk. "Come and join me."

"Do I need to remind you that you're in my space right now? You don't call the shots here, so cut the crap, Cecile. Now, I repeat, what do you want?"

"The first thing we're going to do is get rid of him."

The colossal gall of this woman never ceased to amaze me. "*We* are not going to do anything."

"Oh yes we are, and once you've heard what I have to say, you'll see you have no choice."

I felt my blood pressure rising as every muscle in my body started to tense. It took everything in me to appear relaxed. I would not give this little bitch the satisfaction of thinking she still had an effect on me.

"Say what you've come to say and get out."

"You're going to wish you were a lot nicer to me, Connor, so quit acting like a cheap piece of shit."

You could take the girl out of the trailer park but just couldn't take the trailer trash out of the girl. I stifled the smirk at this sign I was getting on Cecile's nerves and said nothing.

"Fine. Hide behind your little desk if you want. Can you at least offer me a drink?"

"What would you like?"

"You know very well what I like, Connor," she snapped.

I pressed the intercom and asked Stella to bring Cecile a hot chocolate.

"Now, let's not waste any more time. What do you want?"

"Fine. We'll play it your way for now. You're going to give me control of Magnum and the Masquerade clubs, and you're going to marry me."

I stared at her, flabbergasted, then I snorted out a laugh. She had to be kidding. Stella knocked quietly and let herself in with the hot chocolate. I was grateful for the moment to gather my thoughts.

"You must be delusional. Why would I do any of those

things?"

"Because if you don't, you're going to land your ass in jail, and your sweet little slut is going to live out the rest of her life in misery. I'll see to it. She'll make an excellent addition to one of the princes' harems, and you'll never see her again."

Red fury washed across my vision. "And just how do you think you're going to pull this off?" *Play naïve. Bait the trap.*

"Actually, Connor, I've already pulled it off. One call from me, and you and Brett are going to be arrested for international title fraud. I'm sure by this time you've heard there are some irregularities with your books. Well, dig a little deeper, and you'll discover that you've been selling mortgages for rental properties that don't exist."

"That will be relatively easy to disprove. You're going to have to do better than that."

"My partners are very good at what they do, and our inside man has made sure the trail leading back to you is solid. Oh, and it gets better. When the mortgages were paid out, you put the money into a trust account, and you recently withdrew the funds."

"No one is going to believe that. I have more money than I need now. Why would I take a risk like this for more?"

"Give Brett a call right now, and check it out, Connor. The trail is rock solid. But just to be sure, we have your little slut as insurance. Remember the car accident? Too bad she lived through it, and if you want her to stay that way, you'll do what I say. Of course, she may like harem life. One of my nasty Arab princes is just a phone call away." Cecile gifted me with another smug look before examining perfectly polished nails.

The hair stood up on the back of my neck. My pulse jack-hammered through my head.

"I was supposed to be the one driving Tim to the airport. If the accident was intentional, I would have been the target."

"Oh, we knew it was your Katherine driving her Tim to the airport. Stop being so naive. My spies are everywhere. You should know that by now."

"If you think you can take over Magnum and Masquerade, then go for it, but leave Katherine out of this."

"I thought you'd say that, but no go. I want the whole shebang including the status of being your wife. Your corporate movers and shakers won't have anything to do with me without that clout. And besides, I want you. You're the only man I've ever loved." She threw me a pouty look I might briefly have found sultry. "You should get your head out of the clouds and remember just how perfect we were. Together, nothing can get in our way. You need me, and you're going to be mine.

"It's your turn to find out what it's like to be on the submissive side of things. I'm the only one who really knows you, and I find it sad you've lost yourself in such a stupid little romantic interlude. Time to get a grip and remember who you are, Connor. It was you and me working together that got you everything you wanted. We've got history, and that means your little plaything has to go. After all, she'd just be in the way."

"I'll die before I'll let you do anything to Katherine."

"Don't be a fool. Even you can't protect your precious Katherine forever, and that ought to make your decision easy. You'll get over her before you know it. You know I'm right." Speculation replaced the arrogance as she continued to stare me down.

"You will need some time to check my story. I'll give you one week to give me your answer. Meanwhile, I'll be off planning our wedding. Something spectacular, I'm thinking." She stood and winked. "Remember, all it takes is one phone call, and your little Kat will be some evil man's sex slave."

She blew me a kiss and sashayed out of the office.

15

KATHERINE

While Connor was gone, I made good use of the time, finding out just what the hell was going on. Connor and Brian had been sharing secrets ever since Brett's visit. They were entirely too secretive, and something was very definitely up. I couldn't get a word out of Asha at dinner last night, even after plying her with drinks. That woman could sure hold her liquor.

Connor had left a stack of files on his desk, and I'd sifted through them. He detested technology and preferred paper, making it much easier to snoop. I knew he'd be pissed when he found out I'd gone through them, but what did he expect when he left me here on my own with nothing to do? Besides, fresh eyes and all that. If something was brewing, maybe I could help. I was tired of playing the victim.

The files contained deeds to rental properties Magnum purchased in Georgia. I popped onto *Google Street View* to check out the properties and, try as I might, found nothing but swampland. Magnum sold stocks for the properties as part of a real estate income trust. More paperwork showed the properties were managed by a couple of property management firms. Magnum seemed to be their sole customer. *Strange.* There were copies of real estate income trust stocks sold to a bunch of people who bought into the rental properties. It looked as if they were private preferred shares. *That's one way to avoid a securities investigation.*

As I dug deeper, it appeared that Magnum paid these investors their rental income by selling more trust stocks for properties that didn't exist. This whole setup reminded me of something, but what? I couldn't bring it to mind, but I could understand why Connor and Brian were on edge. Neither one of them would ever be involved in something shady, of that I had no doubt. Both of them were righteous and would go batshit at the thought of a hit to their integrity.

I jumped when the phone rang.

"Hello."

"Hey there, Kat, it's me, Asha. Am I catching you at a bad time?"

"No, not at all. What's up?"

"Want to come here for lunch? I've put together one of your favorite ploughman's lunches. Afterward, we can go shopping in Nice and surprise the guys."

"Lunch? What time is it?"

"It's almost one o'clock, silly. What on earth have you been doing this morning?

"I've been looking through these files on Connor's desk. Oh, my God."

"What, what? Are you okay, Kat? What, for Christ's sake?"

My head pounded as the memory came rushing back. It was Kevin Jordan, my old boss at Magnum, who had told me about a scheme just like the one lying before me in these files. He'd been boasting he knew exactly how to pull off a title fraud scheme without getting caught. I'd passed it off as one of his fairy tales being the blowhard that he was, but maybe he hadn't been bragging all along.

"I'm thinking Kevin Jordan is involved in this rental properties thing."

Asha was silent for a moment, and only the sound of rustling papers came through the receiver.

"What makes you think that? He's in editorial and has nothing to do with the real estate division."

"I don't know for sure, but I have a really strong hunch. I think we could prove it for sure if we take a look at his email accounts and follow the money trail. Is there any way you can get us access to his email account? I bet you'll find email linking him to someone in real estate."

"I can do one better than that. I'll get us into his home and work emails. Forget the shopping trip. Get down here as fast as you can."

The line went dead.

I downed a couple of the pills Hannah had prescribed, grabbed the files and hustled down to Asha and Brian's guesthouse. Asha pulled me through the open door.

"Come on, girlfriend. Show me what you've got," she said. "I think you're on to something here."

We spent the rest of the afternoon looking for clues. Asha dug through the layers of wire transfers, trying to trace the recipient of the funds. Once she got me access, I delved into Kevin's email.

"Have you ever heard of someone named Ken Shantz?"

Asha's head jerked up.

"What did you just say?"

"Ken Shantz. Do you know the name?"

Asha let out a sharp breath, leaped up, and looked over my shoulder. I clicked through a series of emails to Ken with cryptic references to the selling of shares and transfers of funds.

"Stop," Asha said.

I stared at the email that caught her attention. "What?"

The note looked similar to the rest we'd seen. "Two new acquisitions. Eleven hundred sold. Need CD to sign. Forward address."

Asha let out a low whistle.

"What is it?" I asked again.

"The bitch is back. Un–fucking–believable. So my Bri was right."

"What do you mean, the bitch is back? Who's the bitch?"

"Cecile DePoulignac, Connor's ex—um—partner. Connor bounced her out on her ass several months ago and told her to get out of Dodge, so to speak. One of his conditions for letting her off without criminal charges was that she stay clear of anything to do with the Masquerade clubs, or Magnum for that matter."

"No kidding. What did she do? Why would he do that?"

Asha opened her mouth as if to speak, then snapped it shut. She sighed and leaned forward. "What she did isn't my story to tell, so all I can tell you is that she betrayed him. As for why he let her walk away"—she let out another deep sigh —"it's because he's too much of a fucking nice guy. Bri told him we hadn't seen the last of her, but Connor tends to think the best of people."

"But he comes across as such a hard-ass, and I'd never want to cross him."

"Oh, Kat, haven't you learned by now that's just the stone walls of his fortress? Behind those thick walls is a heart of gold. He'll never intentionally hurt anyone he's cared for. That's why Bri is such a good foil for him. He'll always err on the side of hitting first and asking questions later."

"That must be awfully hard to live with."

Asha winked. "Not at all. He knows I hit back."

"Sounds like you two are in fisticuffs all the time." I frowned in horror at the thought of living in this kind of turmoil.

"Not at all. We spend much more time making love than war. One thing is for sure, though, we're never bored." Asha laughed. "But then again, neither are you and Connor."

"I'm having trouble marrying the image you paint of Connor with the man I've been getting to know again. Sometimes I feel like I know him on a deep, visceral level, and other times he seems like a stranger with impossibly high standards. When I'm around him, I feel like I'm on the verge of disappointing him because it's impossible to live up to his expectations."

"Honey, there's virtually nothing you could do to disappoint Connor except maybe lie to him. But then that's the problem with you two. Neither one of you seems to understand the depth of the bond you have. Neither of you can commit."

"I know, right? But just when I start to feel like I'm ready for the next step, he pulls back and acts all righteous on me. What's that about?"

"Good, you're remembering more." Asha gave me a warm smile. "Connor always was a moody and stubborn one, but then again, so are you, Kat. You two were destined for each other. So, it pisses me right off that just when you are finding your way back to each other, Cecile drops in to mess things up, never mind Ken Shantz."

"And just who is this Ken Shantz? And don't think I haven't noticed you didn't answer my question about what this Cecile did to Connor."

Asha gave me that smirk I was coming to know well. "Ken is a very nasty man Connor and Brian had a run-in with many years ago. I'd actually forgotten about him, until now. And look here." Asha pointed to several lines on one of the bank statements she'd printed out. "I had to dig deep, but they've planted a trail that leads back to Connor. I bet when I pull the IP addresses for the original transfers, they'll lead right back to Kevin, the bastard, or whoever he's in cahoots with."

"So, what are we going to do now?"

"We're going to peddle our asses to Nice and bring the guys up to speed with what we've found out. Good work, Kat. You'd make one hell of a good detective."

Asha gave me a high five. I couldn't help but beam with pleasure at the compliment.

"Let's go. We'll take Connor's 911."

"Shouldn't we call and let them know we're coming?"

"Nah. Let's surprise them. Better to ask forgiveness."

Something in my gut told me this was not a good plan. I was dead certain Connor didn't like surprises.

Asha slid the Porsche into one of the reserved spots near the entrance to a glass and marble office complex with the words Magnum International prominently displayed near the top of the building. While the security guard signed me in as a visitor, she tapped her foot and repeatedly jabbed the elevator button until it arrived. We rode to the top floor and walked past a number of well-dressed office assistants sitting outside heavy wooden doors, all closed.

Asha marched toward a rather plump middle-aged woman with graying blond hair sculpted like a military helmet.

"Are they in, Stella?" Asha asked without even glancing her way.

"Yes, Asha, but they aren't—"

Stella half rose, but Asha was already through the door. *Rude!* I extended my hand.

"Hi, Stella, is it? My name is Katherine King. I'm so pleased to meet you. I've heard lots of good things about you." I only vaguely recalled hearing her name, but it was the polite thing to say.

She grasped my hand firmly in both of hers. "I'm so very pleased to meet you again, Katherine." Stella's smile was warm and welcoming.

"Is it okay if I go in there?"

Stella looked toward Connor's office door. "I guess we're about to find out."

As I walked in, I heard a hard edge in Connor's tone as he said, "You had no right involving her, Asha."

I stepped forward into a polished office full of wood, chrome, leather, and what looked to be original art on the walls.

"She didn't involve me, Connor. I involved her. And before you get even pissier, I suggest you hear what we have to say. We found out who the mole is and what kind of scam he's running.

"Really? Who?" Brian asked.

"Kevin Jordan," I said. "And he's running some kind of title fraud Ponzi scheme. I don't quite—"

"Enough," Connor said. "What part of 'I don't want you involved' are you not understanding?"

The coldness in his eyes made me take a step back. Now my temper started to ignite. How dared he speak to me as if I were a child?

"Look, Connor—"

"Drop it, Kat."

The anger in Connor's voice sliced through me like a well-sharpened sword. *What the fuck?*

Brian jerked his head at Asha and pointed toward the door. They scuttled out.

I walked over, put my hands on the edge of the rosewood desk, and leaned toward him. We stood like that for a moment, breathing heavily, shooting daggers at each other.

As angry as I was, I still couldn't help admiring the beauty of the chiseled face that housed those plump, oh-so-kissable lips and those eyes that were often the only indication there was a living, feeling being inside that sculptured body.

"Don't you dare speak to me like that again, Connor. I'm not one of your minions, nor am I a child. I apologize if going through your files was out of bounds, but I'm not going to apologize for caring and wanting to help you."

Hands clenched on his blotter, his stormy eyes continued to bore into me for another thirty seconds. Well, two could play that game. I knew the meaning of 'he who speaks first loses.' Finally, he relaxed his fingers, slowly pushed back from the desk, walked around to my side, and pulled me into his arms. His kiss held the soft whisper of surprise. He lifted me onto the desk and touched his forehead to mine.

"I'm sorry, Kat. You're right. I can be a complete and utter bastard sometimes. I'm not as bad as in my youth, but my temper still runs away on me from time to time. I'm mad at the boss and kicking the dog."

"So now I'm a dog, am I?"

"That's not what I meant."

I leaned back and looked up at him. Try as I might, I couldn't keep the merriment from breaking into a full-fledged grin.

"Am I forgiven?" he asked.

"After a kiss like that, you're more than forgiven. Now, before I rip your clothes off right here and now to fulfill my fantasy about office sex, you'd better let me tell you what I found out."

Connor brushed both hands along the sides of my thighs. The ice in his eyes melted into smoldering heat. This time when he kissed me, his tongue teased the sensitive spot on the roof of my mouth, and dampness saturated my panties. I was panting by the time we pulled apart.

"Let's do it over dinner."

"What about Brian and Asha?"

"They're old enough to fend for themselves."

Connor reached over and pressed the intercom. "That's all for today, Stella. I'll see you in the morning."

She answered, her voice oozing competence and efficiency.

"What time shall I expect you, sir?"

"Let's make it ten, Stella, and not a minute before. Take the night off. Oh, and Stella, that's an order."

He grabbed my hand and pushed a button. A panel slid open on the far wall, and we took the private elevator to a rear entrance where the 911 stood waiting.

16

CONNOR

Agitation washed over me like surf rolling into a rocky beach on a windy day. Cecile had me by the balls, and try as I might, I couldn't figure a way out of it without putting Kat in danger. The car accident was all the proof I needed. Cecile would stop at nothing to get what she wanted. I vowed at that moment never to be in a position of weakness like this again.

I considered one plan after another, but all led me to the same conclusion. There was only one way to keep Kat safe from Cecile and Ken until Brian and I could get the witch out of the picture. I knew that as I fought to save her, I might very well lose her, possibly forever. The thought of it nearly broke me, but her well-being meant more to me than life.

Oblivious to the threat looming over her, Kat had been pumped as she told me all about what she'd uncovered the previous day. She was so proud of herself, you'd think she'd solved the mystery of who had killed JFK.

I didn't give a shit about the business stuff. I'd take the rap and resign in a heartbeat. I wasn't concerned about criminal charges; they weren't anything a good lawyer couldn't handle. That, however, wouldn't solve the real problem. I'd sat in stunned silence as she'd regaled me with her findings about 'some guy named Ken Shantz.' Memories of that night twenty years ago, when my first lover Meredith had put on her very public display with him, came rushing back. The slime was a fucking human trafficker, and with his help, Cecile could more than make good with her threats. What had started as a bad dream with Cecile's reappearance turned into a full-fledged nightmare.

I shuddered as I thought of just what would happen to Kat if they decided to turn her over to one of their Middle Eastern friends. I could just imagine one of the princes getting his rocks off destroying the spunk that was the core of Kat's personality. And there wouldn't be a goddamned thing I could do about it. I'd just never see her again. Better to handle things on my terms.

Somehow, I managed to hide the despair coursing through my veins and maintain a pleasant expression for Kat's sake. After dinner, we took a stroll and settled in at the Marc de Café for our evening espresso.

"What's up, C? Why so glum?"

Kat and her damnable intuition. I'd have to do a better job of hiding my feelings.

"Nothing's up, beauty." I reached across the table and tucked one of her curls behind her ear.

"Okay, now I know for sure something's up. You're never affectionate in public. Spill, Connor."

"I was just thinking about how much I love you and how much I appreciate your insights into the title fraud set-up, that's all."

Those intense gold-streaked brown orbs bored into me, and it was everything I could do not to squirm with guilt at the white lie. *And there's worse to come, Connor.* I repressed a shudder at the thought of how I was about to break her heart. *And mine.* Minutes passed, and her gaze never wavered.

"You're staring again, Alley Kat."

"Uh-huh. And your point is?"

"You're making me uncomfortable, but then again, you know that."

"Do I now?" She laughed her deep, rich belly laugh. "I take it from that remark this is something I do often?"

Shit. For a moment, I'd forgotten she still didn't have all of her memory back.

"Yes, and it still makes me uncomfortable."

"Well, suck it up, buttercup. That's what you get when you're as beautiful as you are," she said.

"I don't think of myself that way, and it puts me on the spot."

"Then it's time you start."

Another tear rent through my heart as I recognized yet another thing about her I'd have to live without—that is if my plan worked. I stood up abruptly.

"Come on. Let's get back to the hotel. I have some calls to make before it gets too late."

With a heavy heart, I called Stella asking her to ensure my suite at the Sparkling Crystal Resort was ready and waiting for our arrival. The world-class spa would delight Kat, and her pleasure would give me memories that would hold me for what might be the rest of my life. I wasn't at all certain that our plan to trap Cecile would work. If it didn't, I'd have to cut all ties to Kat to keep her safe. I didn't want to think about that.

"Consider it done, Connor. Would you like me to arrange a limo?"

"No, I'll have Brian set that up. I want to be sure no one can trace my steps. That's one of the reasons I'm taking her away. I'm going off the grid for the next week."

"Very well, rest assured I'll handle things on this end."

"You always do, Stella. You always do."

I stabbed the release button and called Brian and Asha's suite. He answered on the first ring.

"What's up?"

"I'm taking Kat to the Sparkling Crystal Resort for the next week. Stella's making the usual arrangements to take me off the grid. I'd like a limo company that can be relied upon for their discretion. We'll travel under a pseudonym until we know who is leaking information. I want to be sure there is no way Cecile or her minions can trace our whereabouts."

"She'll be pissed, Connor. Are you sure you want to try her patience this way?"

"I don't give a goddamn how pissed she is, Bri. You know what to do."

"Consider it done, Con. Will you be telling Brett where you are?"

"Leave Brett to me. He'll understand."

The four-hour drive was uneventful. I checked email while surreptitiously watching Kat. In short order, she leaned over, admiring the view as we navigated the winding roads into the mountains. Her infectious enthusiasm improved my mood with each passing kilometer. Of course, it didn't hurt that the little minx took every opportunity to brush against my crotch. As we neared the resort, the large crystalline building shimmering atop a granite ridge beside Lake Geneva amazed her.

The resort really was a spectacular piece of architecture. It had taken our architects several years to scout just the right location to build the edifice they envisioned. Housing ten million dollars of Swarovski crystals and every conceivable amenity, it was the envy of the most exclusive list of clientele. Kat was in awe as we walked up to the entrance. I would make this a visit to remember for all time.

Kat *oohed* and *aahed* over the splendor of our penthouse suite. She gushed over the oak and crystal décor, particularly the radiant heating beneath the marble en suite floor, and the electronic toilet that doubled as a bidet. She ran from room to room exploring.

"Can you believe it? There are crystals everywhere. Look, there are even crystals on the backs of the chairs and embedded in the mirrors. And look at this delicate little crystal chandelier over the dining table. So cool. Where did they get all these crystals?"

Her enthusiasm shone a ray of light through the cloud of my despair, and for a moment, I was oblivious to everything but her childlike sense of wonder.

I would have ordered room service, but Kat wanted to people watch in the dining room. I clamped down on the irritation that shot through me. I didn't want to share any of the limited time I had left with her. But she had no way of knowing how very important this time was for us both, and there was absolutely no way I could risk letting her know.

Like most European resorts, dress for dinner required black tie. However, all irritation left when Kat appeared wearing a stunning red gown. I gave her my arm and escorted her to the dining room. The hostess promptly seated us at my private table with its splendid view of the lake and mountains. The sommelier arrived with the wine list, and I deferred to Kat's preference. She opened the wooden cover and scanned through the list.

"Good grief, C, have you seen the prices on this list?"

"Don't worry about the money, Kat. I've got this covered."

"Well, you won't be able to afford this lifestyle for very long if you keep spending money like this."

My practical Kat. Always on the lookout for my well-being. I loved that Kat had no interest in how much money I made, nor was she interested in spending it. She'd always been very clear that she was her own woman and would pay her own way. If I didn't handle this properly, she'd balk.

"I did the owner a favor, and this is payback. The cost of this trip is covered." *And another white lie.* The necessity of lying was unusual for me, and I hoped I'd be able to keep them all straight.

"It must have been one hell of a favor."

The sommelier returned, and Kat entered into an animated conversation with her before choosing a bottle of Château Lafite-Rothschild 2010 from my personal collection. As she left the table, our server appeared with our menus. More interrogation about the dinner options followed before she settled on the chicken supreme with risotto. I jokingly called her high maintenance, but she could care less what I thought. She knew what she liked, and she wasn't willing to compromise. Another of the many things I admired about her. I, on the other hand, was easy and predictable. Steak, baked, and Caesar salad, choices I rarely deviated from.

Once we'd settled into our dinner, Kat turned her X-ray gaze on me, giving me the feeling she could see directly into my soul.

"So, why are we here, C?"

It took an effort for me to meet and hold her eyes. This time I'd tell her the truth, at least most of it.

"I need some time alone with you Kat, away from the hustle and bustle of everyday life. We haven't had time to focus on just us since the accident. I want us to get back to who we are as a couple."

Kat put down her fork and took a sip of her wine.

"And just who are we as a couple?"

"We're two people exploring your propensity for submission and my ability to be your Dom. Recently, we've lost touch with that, and I want us to get back to our explorations without distraction, for a few days, at least."

"So, when do we start?"

I smiled. Always the eager one.

"Let's get through dinner first, Alley Kat. Now tell me, what do you like the most about being with me?" *Emotionally needy much, Con?*

She took another sip of her wine, never shifting her gaze from mine. Her pupils dilated as a series of thoughts, some clearly salacious, sprang through her mind.

"I suppose it's the element of surprise, of not knowing what to expect. Knowing you're there to take care of me runs a close second. With you I feel safe. I haven't always felt that way. And what do you like the most about being with me?"

Everything! I clamped down on another tear ripping through my heart. Although I knew beyond a doubt what it was, I paused a beat before answering.

"I love the way you surrender yourself to me and your sexuality. You make me feel like I'm the only person in your world that matters."

Most women would have balked at me not saying the L-word at a time like this. Not my Kat; she looked proud and pleased. "You are the only person in my world that matters, C."

We walked back to our penthouse suite, Kat with the remainder of her bottle of wine and I with a bucket of ice for my *Pepsi*. I wasn't much of a drinker, and I didn't want anything to dampen the experience with Kat.

Without ado, Kat fired up the sauna, poured a glass of wine, and shed her clothes.

"You are going to join me, aren't you, C?"

Normally I wasn't one for high heat of any kind except that created by natural sunlight while lying on a beach, but I didn't want to miss one minute of opportunity in the short time we had left.

"Right behind you, babe." I took the time to unpack a few toys in anticipation of our evening together before shucking my clothes and joining her.

She lay back on the cedar slabs of the sauna, arms above her head, legs spread wide, skin glistening in the dim light. I sat at her feet and ran a finger through the slick of perspiration coating her thighs, reveling in the beauty of her sex as her clit peeked through the fullness of her nether lips.

"Touch yourself for me." I added a trace of command to my tone.

I felt rather than saw her questioning gaze, but she complied. Closing her eyes, she slowly brought her hands to her breasts, circling the soft swell of the underbelly before moving to her nipples. Her breath caught as she pinched then twisted them, whimpering a little as she arched into the sensation. My God she was beautiful.

I traced the outline of those plump nether lips, taking care to avoid the ripe bud that appeared from under its hood. She strained and wiggled, silently encouraging me toward this sweet spot.

I bent and whispered into her ear, "Show me what you want."

After a moment's hesitation, she slid her hand down her stomach and framed her fully extended engorgement with her index and middle fingers. Sliding them back and forth, she rubbed her clit. *This is new.* I watched fascinated as she increased the pressure and speed.

"Come for me, beauty."

Her eyes flew open, and she opened her left hand toward me.

"Join me, C."

"This is about you, not me, beauty." With effort, I kept my tone quiet, even though the throbbing of my erection matched the pounding of my heart.

"Please, C. Make this about us."

I propped myself so that my head was at the opposite end of the bench so I could watch her come and slowly began to massage the head of my cock. My face tightened with tension. It wouldn't take much to hurl me over the edge, but I wanted my focus on her.

If the eyes glued on the hand working my cock were any indication, watching me turned my Alley Kat on. In turn, my gaze moved from her face to the increased tempo of the fingers framing her clit. Her breathing grew ragged, and her eyes fluttered shut before springing open again. I kept my pace slow and steady. There would be plenty of time for my satisfaction later.

Smoldering heat made the gold streaks in her eyes light up like hot cinders. She was close to the edge, and her face mirrored the tension in mine.

"Now, C, come with me now." She moaned and grew rigid as her climax overtook her.

I groaned as my balls tightened, leaving me helpless, and my own orgasm exploded, semen squirting over my belly in long streams. She curled into me, taking my vibrating cock deep in her throat and sucking every last drop.

I pulled her to me, and we lay sweating together as our heartbeats slowed.

17

KATHERINE

When the heat from the sauna and our passion proved to be too much, we slipped into a huge shower with a heated floor.

"This place is absolutely gorgeous, C. Thank you for bringing me here." I sidled up beside him and slid an arm around his waist. And tried very hard not to look down at his semi-erect cock.

Connor tossed me a brief smile but stayed focused on adjusting the water temperature before hitting the button marked Rain. Visions of Connor's temper igniting when working with anything mechanical popped into my head. Turning to face me with the grin of a conquering hero, he drew me under a waterfall that reminded me of a midsummer thunderstorm.

"You're pretty proud of yourself, aren't you?" I smiled up at him and searched his face for the undertone of tension I sensed.

"You bet ya. For once, I did not need you to figure it out." He squirted bodywash on the mesh sponge and gently washed me from head to toe. He stepped back, never taking his eyes off me while he lathered himself.

"You're so beautiful." He sighed. "I can't get enough of you."

There it was again, a hint of what . . . sadness? But Connor was far too skilled at hiding his emotions to let anything he considered weakness escape. And for him, expressing strong emotion was a weakness.

"You'd better watch it, C. I could get used to this kind of attention."

He sighed again. Something was definitely up.

"What's the matter?"

"Nothing's the matter, babe. I'm just realizing how deeply attached I am to you."

This was a rather strange thing for a man who loved me to say, but something about commitment issues tugged in my memory. I decided not to overthink it for the moment. He pulled me into his arms and kissed me while the water sluiced the soap from our bodies. After spending a long time massaging me with my favorite body lotion, he pulled me into bed to snuggle up against him.

For a moment, panic shot through me as I imagined that something dreadful—although I couldn't think what—was going to happen. It was so unlike Connor to be this demonstrative. I couldn't shake the feeling something was wrong. Then I gave my head a shake. *Stop catastrophizing and enjoy.* I knew I was being an alarmist, but the nagging feeling stayed with me as I slipped into sleep.

We slept late, and I woke ravenous. We washed together at the dual marble sinks, chatting inconsequentially about the many amenities in our suite. Connor was in a playful mood and took every opportunity to touch me while we donned the thick cotton housecoats provided and waited for room service to bring our breakfast. Thank heaven he'd dropped his melancholy mood.

"Did you enjoy last night, beauty?"

"Absolutely, C. Did you?"

Connor laughed and winked. "You have to ask?"

"What part did you like best?"

"Everything," he said. "What part did you like best?"

I took a minute to think about it. How did one respond to that when every single moment with him was so perfect?

"I loved how you came last night in shuddering gasps. You're usually so quiet. That's okay, but I love hearing you involved and lost."

We sat smiling at each other while we ate, each lost in our own thoughts of salacious activity.

"I feel like you're getting me to open doors I've never opened before," I said.

The smile lighting his face made his eyes glow like emeralds.

"Come here." His voice was husky with lust.

"Oh no you don't, C. If I do that, we'll never eat, and I may die of starvation. Besides, we've got all day. What do you want to do today?

"I want to open all of your doors. How about today we explore your deepest, most secret fantasy?"

"Honestly, C, do you want me thinking about sex with you all day?"

"Yes, I do. I love knowing you're thinking about sex all day. You know that excites me."

"You're asking a lot here, Connor. I'll have to give it some thought." My grin let him know I was game.

"Take all the time you need while we're at the spa. We have the facility to ourselves this afternoon."

I'm not sure how he managed it, but we did indeed have the spa all to ourselves. No staff were in sight as we entered the steam and sauna area. Eight or nine wooden doors ringed a waiting area that held a few benches. The spa brochure mentioned a fire and ice experience, and I was eager to try the different temperatures and scents in the many rooms.

As the door closed behind us, Connor slipped off the housecoat and hung it on the hook outside the first sauna. He was stark naked. I gaped. I had my bathing suit on and intended to keep it on and completely ignored the naughty squirt of heat deep in my belly.

"Rest assured, beauty, no one will disturb us this after-noon. I have you all to myself." He crossed his arms and leaned against the wall, watching and waiting . . . and expecting. I knew what he wanted. Sighing in resignation, I removed the housecoat and bathing suit and turned to face him. His eyes lit as he held his hand for me to take.

Oh boy. He was no doubt going to torture me until he'd coerced my deepest, darkest desires from me. And that's exactly what he did as we moved from room to room. He played with my nipples and clit, nibbled my neck, and did all the things he knew would make me beg for release. Relent-less, he continued this sweet torture in the hot tub and indoor pool. I was almost out of my mind with longing as we stretched out on the lounge chairs by the pool.

"Okay, C, enough. I'll tell you what you want to know."

"Start talking."

Connor's face was taut with desire and determination that told me he'd settle for nothing less than full disclosure. I shut my eyes, unsure whether I could admit this truth even to myself. He grasped my chin and turned my face toward him. My eyes flew open at the rough insistence of his touch.

"Here's the deal. I'll take you one step closer to the climax you so obviously crave when you've told me something you've never admitted before."

I struggled to hide the whimper as heat flushed through my body and beads of perspiration lined the bottom of my breasts and creases of my thighs. Wanting to cool the fire, I got up to take a dip in the pool.

"Oh no you don't." Connor's low rough growl sent another jolt of heat through my core. He grabbed my arms and pulled me back down beside him, his strong hands easily encircling my tiny wrists.

"Start talking," he ordered.

I licked my lips, trying desperately to bring moisture to the dryness caused by excited anticipation.

"You're a rich landowner, and I'm a slave girl you've bought at auction. Although attracted by my looks, it's that haughty attitude defying anyone to break me that draws you to me." I stopped, waiting for any indication that he judged me.

Connor played with my breasts, suckling one nipple and then the other until I arched, gasping with need. He gave one final suck before looking at me, heat smoldering in his intense gray-green eyes.

"And?" he asked.

I whimpered again and took a deep breath.

"You have me bathed and brought to you. Your overseer pushes me into your study and says, 'Kneel bitch.' I jerk my arm out of his, and he slaps me in the face. My head snaps back. 'Enough,' you roar. 'I'll deal with you later.' The overseer stomps off.

"You walk around me while I stare at you defiantly. Running a finger down my back, you smile. 'So, little girl, you have a lot to learn about obedience. You will learn to obey me without question. Tonight we'll start with your first lesson.'

"'You can do whatever you want, but you'll never own me.'

"A half smile tugs at the edge of your sensual mouth. 'By the time I'm done with you, you'll be begging me to take you,' you say."

Connor reached down and brushed his lips against mine, barely making contact. I strained to touch them, but he tightened his hold, keeping me a hair's width away. He brushed his hands over my trembling thighs and through my soaking crotch.

"I'm going to let go so you can stand and show me your body. If you disappoint me, I'll fuck you until I come and leave you wanting. I'll make sure you don't come until you give me what I want."

Holy shit. Suddenly, I remembered that orgasm denial was one of Connor's favorite kinks. Determination and desire shone from Connor's eyes with an intensity that almost blinded me. He released my hands and leaned back on one elbow. I hesitated a beat before standing, trembling and trying desperately not to cross my arms over my breasts. Something powerful, more than sex, was happening. Connor intended to push me beyond the limits of any control I usually held onto.

"And?" he asked.

I licked my lips and studied him. Connor couldn't possibly read my innermost thoughts, so I pondered just how much to tell him.

"Not only will you not come, I'll tan your ass until you beg like you've never begged before."

Oh boy. Another wave of intense heat washed through me. Tanning my hide as he so eloquently put it was exactly what I dreamed of.

"That's what he says to me," I whispered.

"That's what who says to you?"

"The owner."

"And then?"

"Then he says, 'We'll start slow and easy.'"

Without a word, Connor stood, tugged on his housecoat, and held out mine. Grabbing my cast off suit, he took my hand and led me back to our suite. Once there, he pulled off my robe and gestured for me to lie on the bed. Again, he watched me with those feral eyes while he discarded his robe and prowled over to the bed. Crawling between my legs, he forced them apart. With a look of intense concentration on his face, he admired my dripping-wet sex. He ran his index and middle fingers on either side of my clit, just as I'd done while masturbating for him. While using his magic hands to tantalize and tease me, he refused to let me move in any way that would bring on an orgasm. Once again, he pushed me to that point where I was swooning with need.

"Continue."

"The owner grabs my jaw and lifts my chin until I look at him. 'First things first, little girl. You need to learn the consequences of disobedience.' He walks over to his desk and picks up a flogger with what looks like narrow leather tails."

Connor reached into the drawer in the bedside table and pulled out a flogger. "Like this?"

I ran my hands over the smooth black tails, scared and excited all at the same time. *Do I really want this?* A little voice deep inside me said, *Yes, yes, yes.* Had I done this before?

"Just like this." My voice was low as I formed the words.

He drew the tails through the juices flowing between my legs.

"How many lashes does he give you?"

Something in his voice gave me pause. How much could I take? How much did I want to take? Then, a stroke of clarity —*I'm afraid of how far I'm willing to go.*

"Fifty," I whispered.

"I'm not convinced. This is your fantasy we're about to make come true, beauty. Now, how many?"

The commitment and love radiating from his eyes steadied me. I knew beyond a shadow of a doubt that I could trust this man, my love. He would not hurt me or push me further than I could go.

"One hundred." This time, my voice rang with confidence.

"And the safe words?"

"Yellow light and red light."

Connor walked over to the window wall and gazed into the mist drifting off the lake into the mountains beyond. I watched in fascination as he flexed his shoulders and stretched his neck. When he turned around, he'd become the owner.

"Trust me, little girl. This will be nothing compared to the whipping I'll give you if you continue to defy me. Now bend over the end of the bed and spread your legs."

The first few strokes stung but were no big deal. The warmth growing on my ass fueled my excitement, and I wanted more. He delivered five, six, seven, and eight with a little more force. Nine and ten packed a punch, and I reared up. He ran his hands over the welts that were no doubt starting to rise.

"Are you willing to obey?"

I shook my head. *Be careful what you ask for, Kat.*

"So you want to play, do you?"

He delivered six more strokes in rapid succession, three on each side. The force made the earlier strapping seem like love taps and brought tears to my eyes. I loved it, and a strange sort of lethargy started to roll through me. The skin burned as he passed his hands over my ass, and I craved the sensation.

"What do you want now, little girl?"

I said nothing and sank further into that place where nothing existed but the sensations flooding my body and this man. I slipped deeper into the fantasy and became his slave. Four more strokes followed. My back arched with the painful pleasure as each one landed.

"Where are we?" His fingers caught in my hair, and he yanked my head back. Good thing, because my head was too heavy to hold up on its own. "Open your eyes, little one."

I forced them open. Studying my eyes, he said, "Check-in time. Where are we?"

"Green, sir." *Oh, so green.*

Connor let my head drop before releasing my hair. I shivered as the room's air hit where his heat had fired my body.

"And now? Are you ready to submit?" He swished the flogger in the air.

"I will never submit to you."

"Have it your way, little girl." He used the flogger like an artist's brush, painting designs over my skin until my juices ran like a river down the insides of my thighs.

Every several strokes, he stopped and ran his hands over my skin, checking in. Each time, I squirmed for more, only vaguely aware when I started to beg. "Take me, goddammit. You're going to anyway." Because part of the fantasy for this slave girl was pushing her master's buttons.

"Pardon?" His voice was gruff with raw desire that matched mine.

"I want you to fuck me hard, master."

"That's my girl, but we're not done here." Flipping me onto my back, he spread my legs wide. Kneeling, his breath hot on my cunt, he inhaled deeply. Sighed with pleasure. He licked between my swollen lips once before latching onto my clit. Sucking with deep pulls, he thrust two fingers deep and pressed into my G-spot. Everything stopped, suspended as each nerve ending froze. Then I came with a force that consumed my body.

As orgasmic contractions shattered me, he drilled into me, his rock-hard shaft filling my hungry cunt, driving the unbearable pleasure to new heights. I screamed with ecstasy as he buried his cock in me again and again. Wave after wave of the most powerful orgasm I'd ever experienced erupted through me. Connor withdrew.

As I lay on the bed panting, he spread a blanket on the cowhide lounger facing the window wall and then placed me on it. Poised above, he looked deeply into my eyes as he slid into me and started a new rhythm, this time slow and sensual. Pulling out until the head of his cock barely teased my opening, he submerged his hard cock a millimeter at a time. Sensation consumed me, and mere seconds passed before I exploded in another paroxysm of pleasure as he took me and owned me.

His breath whispered in my ear. "I love you. I want you. I need you. I can't get enough of you."

I grabbed the cheeks of his ass, grasping. "Take me now. Hard."

But Connor only marched to a master's drum. More slow, torturous strokes stoked the fire yet again and built to a crescendo. He took me to the crest and stood me there. Forced me to reach deep inside and recognize I wanted more. Panting and moaning, I shook with the need to give myself to him again. But this time, I'd break through that wall of control that he held. I made myself watch him, intent on seeing that moment when he let go.

As if sensing my need, he rolled onto his back, taking me with him, cock firmly seated in my cunt. Making me the driver. Left hand on his chest as an anchor, I reached around with my right and grabbed his balls. A low growl escaped from deep within his chest as I clamped my vaginal muscles around his cock and started to ride. Like him, I took my time, setting my own pace, watching him intently. He stared back, letting me see him vulnerable. Finally, moaning, he grabbed my hips and drove up into me. Hard. His eyes closed, and with a deep, feral moan, he exploded into me.

I joined him, and he held me as if he'd never let go as we rode over the cliff together.

18

CONNOR

Reality hit home fast and hard when I woke the next morning. I was a real prick. This beautiful, perfect woman had exposed her innermost thoughts to me, and I was about to reward her trust with betrayal. I had three days before I had to give Cecile my answer—three days I had intended on spending with Kat. But after last night, I could no longer ignore the nagging guilt at hiding the truth from her. With my usual gift for denial, I ignored the inner voice poking at me about my commitment issues. There'd be time enough to deal with that guilt later.

I grabbed my cell and went down to the coffee shop to be sure of privacy. I didn't want Kat to overhear as I made the arrangements.

"Hi, Con. What's up?" Brian picked up on the first ring.

"I'm coming back to Nice today. Arrange to have the jet refueled and ready to take off for home tomorrow."

"Talk to me, buddy. What's going on? I thought this was going to be your big hoorah, so you could get her back once this is all over. Now you're cutting it short?"

I sighed as I clamped down on the frustration overtaking

me. I was a very private person and preferred to hold my cards close, even from Brian, but Kat's needs came before my sensibilities.

"I was, but we had a moment last night, and she got to me, Bri. I can't take another day with her, or I'll never be able to let her go. It's tearing me apart."

I shouldered the cell phone and ran my fingers through my hair. I didn't want to open myself to the agony I felt at the thought of never seeing her again. I clamped down on the emotion. *Keep it strictly business. The business of keeping Kat safe.*

"I think you'll agree the only way I can be sure Kat comes to no harm is to send her home, while I pretend to go along with Cecile's plans," I said.

"Yes, I agree. That should buy us the time we need to nail the bitch. I don't see Katherine going peacefully, though. You know she's not going to leave you while she thinks you're in danger, especially not when she gets her memory back."

"Which is why it's critical she believes I want her out of the way before she gets the rest of her memory back."

Brian whistled. "The rest. That changes things, my friend. What do you need from me?"

"Book a meeting with Cecile and have Asha meet us at the hotel so she can take Kat back to the villa to pack up the rest of her belongings. If we leave here before noon, we should arrive there around four or five this afternoon or even a little earlier if traffic moves well. You and I will stay at the suite in Nice. I need to get my head together before I meet Cecile tomorrow. I'll need to be at my best to convince her. She'll be looking for any cracks in my armor."

"You know Katherine's going to want to go with you, and Asha's not going to be too happy with an angry mountain lioness to handle."

"She's up to it, Bri. I'll make sure Kat is ready to pack and go back to Toronto. But yes, Asha may have to deal with the backlash. I don't care what she does as long as she gets Kat on that plane."

"Leave it to me. Good luck, Con."

I clicked off and ordered a coffee, double cream, double sugar. Staring off into the morning mist, I tried to get a grip on my emotions. Every cell in my body yearned to stay here in this mountain paradise with Kat forever. I loved her with every fiber of my being but knew that love just wasn't enough. I had to keep her safe from the predators. Nothing else mattered.

I was far from an aggressive guy, but I wanted to punch something. Or someone—Cecile's face sprang to mind. But physical violence was more Brian's style. I was a lover, not a fighter. If I was going to beat Cecile, I'd have to do it with brain power. First, I needed to convince Kat I didn't want her with me anymore. I finished my coffee, squared my shoulders, and went back to the suite to face my future. It was the last thing I wanted to do. It was tearing me apart. *What choice do I have?* No choice at all.

Kat ran to me as I opened the door.

"There you are, my lover. I wondered where you were."

She rose on tiptoes to give me a kiss I couldn't accept, or I'd break. I grabbed her shoulders and moved past her.

"Get your things together, Kat. We're leaving within the hour."

"Why? What's happened? After last night, I thought—"

"You thought what?"

I had to avoid the startled hurt that sprang into her eyes, or I wouldn't go through with the plan. I pulled my suitcase from the bedroom closet and started packing.

"Don't just stand there, Katherine. Start packing."

"What the fuck, C. I don't understand." She marched up to me and snatched the pants I'd folded out of my hands. "Stop this right now and tell me what is going on."

"Nothing is going on. I got called back to Nice on business, and it's something I need to take care of free of distraction. I need to focus, so I don't need you around, Kat. You'll be going back to Toronto as soon as you've packed up your belongings at the villa." I forced the bite into my tone.

"Okaaay."

I could almost see the wheels turning as she dragged the word out. "I get it. Something serious happened with your business that you need to take care of. What can I do to help?"

"The best help you can give me is to go home."

She thinned those pretty lips and stared at me for a beat. I knew this woman. She wouldn't beg, she'd just plot and plan a way to maneuver around me.

"Connor, I'll ask you one more time. What's going on? This isn't like you. Especially after last night."

"This is *exactly* like me. Last night was a little interlude of frivolity, and today it's back to the real world. I've got a business empire to run, and I've been distracted from it for far too long."

"A. Little. Interlude. In. *Frivolity*?"

Good. I was finally getting through to her.

"That's what I said. You women are always trying to read something more into things. It was sex, Kat, pure and simple." I spoke the words I knew would seal my fate.

"So, I'm an emotional misfit who is *distracting* you from your business, am I? Well, fuck you too, Connor."

She threw my pants in my face and stomped into the living room where she serenaded me with the slamming of cupboard doors and drawers. Part of me wanted to run to her and hold her and never let her go. I steeled myself for what I had to do, praying that once the threat to her was past, I'd get her back.

When she was done, Kat pulled the suitcase to the door and stood glaring at me.

"Well, come on then, Connor. After all, you're in such a goddamn hurry. Let's go. I'll be in the lobby."

She struggled to get her case through the door.

"Kat, you don't need to take that. I'll call the bellhop—"

"I don't need your help, thank you very much."

The unsaid *asshole* rang in my ears as the door slammed behind her.

***

Kat hadn't said more than twenty-five words since we left the hotel. Who could blame her? She was probably thinking I was a royal bastard. If I asked her a question, she answered very politely. She'd studiously ignored me and looked out the window, staring into the mountain mist. I could tell by the look on her face she was plotting something, but I was one step ahead of her. Asha wouldn't let her out of her sight until she was back on the plane headed for Toronto.

I took out our Double Diary and scanned through our entries. Before the accident, I'd proposed that we write each other our hopes, dreams, thoughts, and fantasies as a way of getting to know each other on a deeper level. Kat had eagerly embraced my suggestion, and the diary had become a way for me to communicate feelings I couldn't verbalize. My gut twisted as I read what she'd written this morning. *She remembered.*

Double Diary

Katherine on September 17 @ 7:50 a.m.

My love! How precious you are to me. How I loved last night and our slave girl fantasy. Who knew I could be that wanton and abandoned? Only you can uncover what I've hidden from myself.

Speaking of hiding, remembering this diary is quite a lovely surprise. I love it!

I can't wait to see what you have in store for us today. Of course, I do have some hotel fantasies we can explore—mistress, call girl, nooners, same time next year—you have many to choose from.

Do hold or tie me down again, please. I love the gentle and loving, but I also love the demanding and dominating sex. I'm feeling in this mood . . .

God, you excite me. Intimately yours forever! ~Kat

How did I respond to that? I wanted to leave her with something, give her something to hang on to. Something that would bring her back to me after I'd cleared up this predicament with Cecile and that scumbag Ken.

Kat looked over and scowled when she saw the diary. She opened her mouth as if to ask for it, then clamped her lips shut. *Oh no you don't, babe. At least not until I give you something to consider.* I pulled out a pad and started writing.

~~Kat, I love you. I know that's hard for you to believe right now.~~

~~You know I come with a lot of baggage, and I've got to take care of this business trouble before I'm free to be with you.~~

~~Sending you home isn't about my fear of losing you, it's about keeping you safe.~~

.   .   .

I kept on like this, scribbling and scratching out. The right words just wouldn't come to me.

"Sir."

I looked up as the dividing window slid down.

"I'm about to stop for petrol, sir. Is there anything you need?"

Good lord. Two hours and I still hadn't figured out what to write.

"Nothing for me, thanks, Bernie. Anything for you, Kat?"

She peeled her lips back over her teeth in what anyone who didn't know her might have mistaken for a smile.

"No thank you, Connor. I have everything I need right here."

Fuck. Would Asha need to physically put her on the plane? I didn't envy her one little bit; but then, that's why she made the big bucks. In truth, like Brian, she was a friend first who would do anything for me, and I needed their help now more than ever.

A text from Brian popped into my cell phone. "Meeting with the bitch moved. Tomorrow at noon. Lunch. Her idea. Les Sens."

Of course, she would pick the best restaurant in Nice to gloat over her conquest. *Bitch!* I would deal with her tomorrow. Right now, I needed to focus on my message to Kat.

I scribbled and scratched, drawing a line through each heartfelt word. *Damn it!* Why couldn't I come up with what I needed to say?

~~I'm so sorry I hurt you.~~

~~I didn't want to hurt you.~~

~~I treasure that you shared your innermost~~

. . .

Finally, I came up with something I was satisfied with and copied it into the Double Diary. Now all I had to do was find a way to get it into Kat's luggage so she didn't see it until she was back in Toronto.

The limo glided up to the front entrance of the Hotel Royal Riviera. Brian pulled up in the 911 with Asha directly behind in the Mercedes. Asha got out and hugged each of us in turn. Brian stepped out of the Porsche and busied himself paying the limo driver, while Asha transferred Kat's overnight bag to the Mercedes. Kat and I stood around, waiting for one of us to make the first move.

"So, what's the plan?" Kat asked.

"Asha will take you back to the house to pack. Brian and I will stay here and take care of business," Connor said.

"And that's it? You stay, and I go?"

Kat's eyes brimmed with tears. I could barely stand to look at her. I reached over and touched her hair, the silky black curls slipping through my fingers.

"What do you want from me, beauty?" My heart tore just a little bit more at what this was doing to her. She looked at me for a long moment.

"Nothing. Absolutely nothing." She reached up and touched my cheek. "Goodbye, Connor."

She slid into the passenger seat of the Mercedes, and Asha drove away. I kicked the 911's tire repeatedly before getting in and driving to the office. Cecile would pay for this.

19

KATHERINE

"What the fuck is going on, Asha?"

"What do you mean?"

"Cut the crap. You know everything Brian knows. Why the fuck won't anyone talk to me?"

"Look, Kat. I'd love to tell you what I know, but I can't. I'm bound by the terms of a very strict confidentiality agreement, besides which, I'd betray Connor's trust if I told you."

I brooded for a moment, then sighed loudly and deeply. I was on my own. As usual. Good thing I'd taken a peek at Connor's phone while he'd taken a pit stop in Turin. At least now I knew where he was running off to and why—he was following some lead on the title fraud business. That annoyed me even more. It was Asha and I who identified the bogus real estate deals, and it just wasn't fair to cut us out now. There just *had* to be something I could do to help him.

"Okay, I get it. I won't give you a hard time. This isn't your fault."

Asha blew out a breath. "Thanks for understanding."

We drove along in silence while I looked into the bright

sky and contemplated my next move. How was I going to give Asha the slip tomorrow?

"You hungry?" Asha asked.

"No, I ate on the plane, but I don't mind stopping if you want something to eat?"

"Nope, I'm good."

No chance there.

"What's the plan for tomorrow?"

"You'll pack, and I'll take you back to the airport in the morning. Connor's orders."

I needed to do something to delay that trip to the airport. *What to do? What to do?*

"We can make a couple of stops on the way to the airport, can't we?"

"What kind of stops?" Asha sounded suspicious.

"There are a couple of things I saw in Nice that I'd like to pick up, and I want to take some of those wonderful little cakes with the crusty crust back with me. I don't think I'll find them at home. After all, I have no idea when or if I'll ever get back here again, and it's not like the jet has to leave at any particular time."

"Oh, you mean *kouign-amann.*" Asha laughed. "For sure, you probably won't find them in Toronto, and even if you did, they won't taste the same."

"Exactly."

"You do love your shopping, don't you? I guess it won't hurt to take a little detour."

I felt kind of bad for tricking Asha, but a woman had to do what a woman had to do.

Asha pulled up in front of the villa and put the car in park.

"I'll take your suitcase in for you?"

"You coming in for a nightcap?" I asked.

"Not unless you need me to. I think I'll get some shut-eye. It's going to be a busy day tomorrow."

You don't know the half of it.

Asha left the suitcase in the hallway. I pulled it into the bedroom, opened it, and scattered a few clothes on the bed just in case prying eyes decided to drop by. I never knew what Connor had up his sleeve, and I wouldn't put it past him to have Asha check on me.

I poured myself a glass of wine and took it into Connor's office, hoping to find something that would help him out of this mess. I tapped the keyboard, and the request for a password came up. I took a sip of wine. What would he use? From what I knew of Connor, he didn't like complicated, so the password was probably something straightforward. Dare I hope it had something to do with me? *Of course you do, silly goose.*

I tried Kat. Nothing.

I tried beauty. Nothing.

Shit. I sure hoped this wasn't one of those computers set up to freeze on too many incorrect attempts.

I keyed in AlleyKat. Bingo, the home screen sprang to life. I laughed out loud. For someone who liked to peg himself as unpredictable, Connor was, well, kind of predictable.

I took another sip of wine for inspiration. The problem was, I had no fucking idea what I was looking for. Being the curious little Alley Kat I was, I decided to start with his pictures. Maybe they would give me some ideas. Connor wasn't much of a photographer, so I didn't think there'd be many of them, but you never knew with people.

As expected, the first few subfolders contained pictures of his cars—looked as if he had quite the collection—a couple of yachts and a few jets. There were quite a few pictures in the yacht folder, some with people on them. I sat forward. Now people could be interesting. Besides Brian and Asha, I had no idea who Connor's friends were.

The first few looked like business contacts and their wives. Nothing twigged there. I continued to scroll and was about to give up when a picture of Connor with his arm around an absolutely stunning woman filled the screen. I stared into violet eyes. *Just like Liz Taylor. Liz.* No that wasn't it, but something about her nagged at me.

I scrolled around a while longer without success. I was about to go into his email when a bolt of guilt hit me. My hand froze on the mouse. If I went into his email, I'd definitely be intruding on his privacy. No, I couldn't do that. No sirree. Besides, he might be able to tell someone was in there, depending on how he had his preferences set up.

A better idea would be to look for paper files. I turned my attention to his desk, carefully rummaging so as not to disturb the contents. I hit pay dirt in drawer number three. I pulled out a thick file labeled Cayenne Accident. *Now this might prove interesting.*

The first few pages were police reports about the initial investigation into an accident. *My accident.* Now the file had my attention. I flipped through the next few pages until the words *Accident Cause* leaped up at me. *Oh my God.* I could feel the niggle of a headache threatening, but I ignored it. I pulled out the stack of pictures, and a pair of dead eyes stared up at me. *Tim!*

And it all came rushing back. Pain shot through my head. I grabbed my temples and moaned. Rocking didn't help. *Have to lie down. Stop the pain.* I stumbled to my feet. The breaking glass behind me barely registered. Somehow, I made it to the bed and collapsed onto it. Darkness descended.

I opened my eyes a slit, memory of the pain my first thought. The dawn light was filtering through the sheers. *Shit . . . 6:34 a.m.* Gingerly, I sat up. The pain was gone; my memory was not. And now I knew. Tim was dead. *Tim was dead.* But mourning for him would have to wait. Somehow, Cecile, my accident, the title fraud stuff, Ken and Kevin, they were all related. I wasn't sure exactly what Connor had gotten himself into, but I was sure as hell going to do everything in my power to get him out of it.

Suddenly, I knew exactly what I had to do.

I was ready and waiting when Asha arrived around eleven o'clock. I'd dressed in jeans, a turtleneck, sweatshirt, and runners. After all, I was returning to Toronto—ha ha—where the fall weather would warrant this apparel. I dragged the suitcase to the car. Asha hefted it into the trunk before giving me the once-over.

"Are you okay?" she asked.

"I'm great. Why do you ask?"

"Something looks different about you. I can't quite put my finger on it."

"Huh. Not sure what that would be." I climbed into the passenger seat. "Let's head to the Rue du Pont Vieux. There's a cute little restaurant there that sells *kouign-amann.*"

I buckled my seat belt and sat back for the ride, reminding myself not to do anything to raise Asha's suspicions.

"Are you feeling better this morning?"

Better?

"What do you mean by better?"

"You were pretty upset with Connor last night. I thought you might still be angry with him."

"Oh, I am still pissed with him, but I realize he's doing what he thinks is right in his alpha-male-lordship way. Besides, it's time I got back to figuring out where things are at with my life, and I can't do that from here."

"Won't that be hard to do without your memory?"

"I'm assuming I'll have bank records and such at home. With any luck, I'll find the name of my accountant and lawyer and start there."

"Let me know if we can do anything to help. I imagine we'll be going home soon as well."

Should I be interested or sound neutral?

"Oh? How soon?"

"As soon as Connor's cleared up this business problem. You know he'll be dying to get back to you, Kat. Oh, here we are," Asha said. "Do you want me to drop you while I find a place to park? Looks like it's getting busy in there."

"That would be good. I have to pee like crazy. I'll ask for a table and take a pit stop. I'll put it under your name to make it easy."

"Okay, see you in a minute."

Hopefully, that would buy me the time I needed. I rushed out the back of the restaurant and sprinted over to the taxi stand at the corner. Thank God there was a taxi waiting there. I got into the back seat.

"Drive."

The driver turned around to stare at me. *"Pardon? Où?"*

"Just drive, dammit. I'll give you the address in a minute."

"Oui, madam." He pulled away from the stand and moved into the lunch-hour traffic.

I dug in my purse for my phone. "Ah, here it is. Take me to Les Sens restaurant on Rue Pastorelli."

A few minutes later, he pulled up in front of a modern building with white lettering on a purple awning. Inside, the decor was a delightful combination of wood and brick, augmented by a large granite-topped bar. Thankfully, the maître d' was nowhere in sight. I paused for a moment to let my eyes adjust from the bright noon light and get my bearings. Connor sat at a corner table with his back to me. Cecile looked directly at me and smiled. *Game on.* I strode over to the table.

"Well, well," Cecile purred. "If it isn't your little kitty cat. Doesn't she know how to take no for an answer?"

Connor sprang to his feet, confusion and fear lighting his handsome features. "What are you doing here? You're supposed to be on your way home." He gave me a hard look that I chose to ignore. "This is no place for you."

Cecile stood, sidled up beside Connor, and looked up at him.

"Some people never learn, do they?" Cecile turned her cold violet gaze on me. "Well, see for yourself, he's mine now, honey. He's back where he belonged in the first place."

I looked back at her with a coldness I'm sure matched her own.

"Back the fuck off, Cecile. This is between Connor and me."

Cecile let out a sound that might have qualified as a laugh. "Kitty cat remembers who I am. Even better. Tell her, Connor."

Awareness lit Connor's eyes. Then something else slithered through them. He squared his shoulders and slid an arm across Cecile's shoulders.

For a split second, I stood frozen to the spot, then blinked rapidly. *This can't be happening. She must have some kind of hold over him.* I held his gaze.

"May I speak to you in private?"

"Anything you have to say to me you can say in front of Cecile, Katherine." His voice was cold, distant. Never, even in his worst mood, had I heard Connor sound so remote.

"Fine. I know you want me to go home to keep me safe, but I can help you. I don't know what she has on you, but we can deal with it together. We can deal with anything as long as we're together, but you have to trust me. I know what you've been dealing with, and I can help you put the pieces together." I bled every ounce of passion I had into my tone. *Hear me. I remember. Read between the lines, C.*

"Connor? What is she talking about? Should I be giving Ken a call?" Cecile moved to pull out her cell phone.

"That won't be necessary," Connor said. Something dark and unfathomable crossed his eyes. "Apparently, I didn't make myself clear, Katherine. Trying to let you down easy was a mistake. We're through. I'm with Cecile now."

"Just like that? After what she's done to you?"

"Just like that. She explained all that, and we're good now." Connor tightened his arm around Cecile and looked down at her. "Aren't we?"

My eyes grew wide of their own accord as he leaned down and kissed those ruby-red pouty lips. She opened her mouth, offering her tongue, and he accepted the offer.

I closed my eyes, counted to three, and opened them again. Bile rose like the gush of a geyser. Yes, it was really happening. Connor was tonguing the bitch while he stared right at me. I tried to absorb the shards of agony shooting through me. I would not beg.

I straightened and stared right back at him. "Your loss," I mouthed, then turned and walked out.

20

CONNOR

Misery sliced through me as I watched that pretty little ass walk through the door, perhaps for the last time. I had my doubts whether my Alley Kat would be able to forgive me after the little display I'd just put on for her. It was everything I could do to keep from pushing Cecile away from me as I took a step back.

"Ah, what's the matter, shoogums," Cecile purred. "Don't worry about her. You'll forget her in no time."

"Understand me clearly, Cecile." I put the sharpened edge of a double-edged sword into my tone. "You are never to refer to Katherine again. Never. If I ever hear her name cross your lips again, all bets are off."

As soon as the words left my mouth, I knew I had to rein in my emotions. I took a deep breath.

"Look, Cecile, I gave a lot of thought to what you've said, and I have to admit in many ways you're right. We don't need Katherine to complicate things, so let's just get things back to the way they should be and leave her out of it."

"Fine, fine. You don't have to be so bitchy about it. You need me in your life, and it's only a matter of time before you realize this. No one will ever love you the way I do. Now, let's finish our business so we can consummate this deal."

I shuddered at the thought of fucking Cecile but almost felt sorry for her. She'd actually been quite delightful when I first met her, tacky attitude and all. But then she'd scented money and the lifestyle she'd always craved. Trouble was, it had been so long since the woman beneath the greed had surfaced, I wasn't sure she was in there anymore. Even worse, she actually believed what she felt for me was love. *Pathetic.*

And then there was my Alley Kat. Kat's love was an action that she showed with each breath she took. She'd stood there all brave and fierce and belligerent and strong, challenging anyone to stand in the way of protecting me. Oblivious to danger, even with her memory back. For her, I was her world and Cecile no longer existed. I'd almost caved and gone to her, but I couldn't risk it. Wouldn't risk it. Cecile and her minion posed too big a threat to Kat's safety.

"I hear your Kat gave Asha the slip and confronted you and Cecile at the restaurant? I'm sorry, man. Asha feels terrible." Brian sat down opposite me and slid some files across my desk.

"Tell her not to," I said. "Kat's as smart as a whip, and nothing will deter her once she sets her mind on an end goal. There's probably not much Asha could have done to stop her. I wonder how she found out where I was meeting Cecile?"

"She told Asha she looked at your phone while you stopped for coffee in Turin."

"How was she? Did she cry?"

I held out the faint hope that maybe, just maybe, she'd

seen through my ruse and trusted I was doing the best for her, for us.

"No, that's the thing, Con. Asha says she was just very matter-of-fact, very cold. Whatever you did with Cecile convinced her, man. It's going to take one hell of a lot of talking for you to get her back. This time, you'd better get past your commitment terror and get ready to take the deep dive."

I grimaced, knowing he was right. Time enough to think of that later. "Then let's get to it because I don't know how much longer I can stand this. I can't get the hurt on Kat's face out of my mind, and every time I look at Cecile, I want to wipe that smug expression right off her face. I hope you brought me something that will help us do just that. What have you got for me?" I opened the file and whistled as I looked through the affidavit taken from Kevin Jordan.

"How did you get this?" I asked.

"Actually, you can thank your Kat for that. That guy is such a blowhard and doesn't know when to keep his mouth shut. When she remembered his story, I gave Brett a call. Brett put the screws to him. It didn't take long for him to be singing like a bird."

"Is it everything we need?"

"That along with the money trail Kat and Asha found was enough to point Razor and his Interpol team in the right direction. He says that money trail helped him connect Cecile and Ken with the human trafficking trade. He's had them under surveillance, and Ken's still up to his old tricks, he's just refined them a little. And lastly, we have the testimony of the housekeeper. She confirms making the phone calls to let Cecile know your whereabouts."

I frowned. "I wish we had some hard evidence that they were responsible for the crash."

"I'm confident Razor's team will find the evidence we need when they search their premises."

"So what happens next?" I jumped up and paced the length of my office. I wanted this over with, right now.

"Razor expects to have warrants for their arrest by noon tomorrow. He wants to make sure they have no wiggle room. He's agreed to wait until they've signed the contract before he arrests them. Once Cecile and Ken sign it, we've got them."

"Cecile will never sign a contract that will implicate her."

"She will if she thinks it's for her protection. You'll just have to be convincing. You know she's not all that bright, Con."

It had taken a lot of talking and allowing Cecile to fawn all over me during dinner the previous evening, but I'd finally convinced her I'd drafted a contract she'd be more than happy with giving her control of Magnum, and Ken control of the Masquerade clubs. Now that the time was near, I could barely sit still. I just wanted this to be over so I could be on my way back to my Alley Kat.

"Let's go over it one more time," Brian said.

"I'll play the whipped puppy—"

"Don't simper too much or she won't believe it."

"Right. Whipped, but not beaten. Got it. I'll order a drink to toast our new partnership, and even though I'll probably gag, I'll be cordial to Ken."

"And I won't punch him. At least not yet." Brian smiled.

"I'll give each of them a copy of the contract and offer to take them through it. Cecile will make noises about needing a lawyer, and I'll let her know I have one standing by."

"The suitcase of money I'll be holding will be incentive for the greedy little bitch."

"That should put the icing on the cake, no doubt. Anyway, I'll make a point of mentioning there's no escape clause in the contract," I said.

"Adding that clause about the contract being irrevocable was a stroke of genius on your part. Once Razor sees them sign the contract, he'll come in with the warrants and make the arrest."

"You're sure this will stick?" I was petrified they'd escape, that I'd never be free from Cecile's clutches, and Kat would never be safe.

"I'm sure. Razor knows what he's doing, and they fucked around with the wrong people when they broke international law."

"Then let's get this show on the road."

Later that day, and right on cue, Cecile flounced into Les Sens with Ken in tow. I'd chosen her favorite to increase her comfort level. Ken's red head, now streaked with gray, towered above hers. I'd forgotten just how large he was. But I, however, was no longer the naive young man half out of his mind with lust and puppy love. Razor sat quietly at an adjacent table, just another customer enjoying his lunch.

I rose and let Cecile walk into my arms and kiss me. Did they make an antiseptic mouthwash strong enough to get rid of her stench?

"And you remember Ken, don't you, sweetie," Cecile said, clutching my arm. "He tells me you've already met. What a small world." Cecile giggled.

"That was a long time ago. Ken." I turned to the man and

shook his hand, barely managing to hide my hatred for him. "You remember Brian?"

"Oh yeah, the little man," Ken said. "What is he doing here?"

"Where I go, he goes," Brian said.

"Not for long," Cecile muttered.

"Fine but he has your money." I pointed to the two suitcases. "A half a million dollars each as a signing bonus. That should keep you going until ownership can be transferred."

"Let's see," Cecile said.

Brian hefted each case on the table and opened one then the other. Bright shiny new hundred-dollar bills sat lined up in neatly bound stacks.

"Dollars? What the fuck are we going to do with Canadian dollars in Europe?" Ken growled.

"We'll exchange them, darling. You know what they say? Don't sweat the small stuff," Cecile said. She took a seat at the table. "Come on. Let's get on with it."

Ken sat down beside her, and for a moment, I wasn't sure I'd be able to go through with this. Brian's solid presence steadied me. I put out my hand, and Brian placed the two contracts in it. I gave one to each of the scum sitting across from me.

They each riffled though the papers.

"Looks like a lot of legalese to me," Ken said.

"Let me take you through it." I explained what each section contained, glossing over the section where they incriminate themselves.

"The principles identified herein would forfeit any claim to the agreed to contract subject to inherent and established business practice including any breach to accepted standards, legal or otherwise, not in keeping with the company's mandate."

"Huh? What the fuck does that mean?" Cecile demanded.

"To put it simply, Magnum and Masquerade will operate above board as they always have."

"No problem," Cecile said.

"Take some time and read these clauses," I said. "They make the terms of this agreement irrevocable. Once we all sign this, Cecile, you own the controlling share of Magnum, and Ken owns the Masquerade clubs. As agreed, I'll remain as CEO." I almost choked on the words.

"Irrevocable. I like that," Cecile said. "Where's the pen?"

"Don't you think we should have a lawyer look this over?" Ken threw me a look dripping with venom.

"Shut up, Ken. I know just as much as any lawyer does, if not more. Didn't you hear him? It's irrevocable. Where do I sign?"

"We'll need a witness to your signatures," I said.

"Can't Brian do it?" Cecile asked.

"It needs to be someone at arm's length. Ah, perhaps this gentleman will help us?" I gestured to Razor as he walked toward us.

Brian stepped over to him.

"Sir, could I trouble you for a moment of your time? I'm wondering if you'd witness the signatures of my friends here. We'd be happy to buy you a drink for your trouble."

"No problem at all." Razor walked over to the table and shook hands. "Razor Ramirez, at your service."

I walked them through initialing each page and placing the final signatures where indicated by the *Post-it* arrows. A copy for them and a copy for me. What seemed like eternity finally ended. Brian double-checked the signatures while I made a toast.

"Here's to our future." I raised my glass.

Cecile took a gulp and thumped her glass on the table. "Now, where's my money?"

"First you'll need this." Razor placed an arrest warrant

into her outstretched hand. Next, he pulled Ken's wrist and dropped one onto his palm. Several men approached the table and stood silently beside it.

"What the fuck is this, and who the fuck are they?" Ken waved the warrant in Razor's face.

"You're under arrest for murder, attempted murder, title fraud, money laundering, blackmail, and human trafficking. It is my duty to inform you that you have the right to retain and instruct counsel in private, without delay. You are not obliged to say anything, but anything you say . . ."

Ken jumped up, and glasses went skittering across the table. Brian's fist met Ken's gut, and he doubled.

"I've been wanting to do that for over twenty years. Little man, my ass," Brian said.

Razor finished reading Cecile and Ken their rights while his men quickly cuffed them. The look on her face was price-less. Her face twisted with rage as she spat out the words, "You fucking double-crosser. I'll get you for this if it's the last thing I do. These charges are bogus."

"The charges prove you've been doing anything but holding to established business standards. Your illegal actions render the contract null and void. Irrevocably." I smiled at the stunned look on Cecile's face as the meaning of the clause in the contract slowly penetrated. She cursed and threatened everyone as they dragged her out the door, spitting and fuming all the way.

"Thank you for your help, gentlemen. That should be the last you see of those two. When we're done with them, the Saudis want their piece. I almost feel sorry for them." Razor smiled.

Brian clapped him on the shoulder. "Thank you, my man. We couldn't have done it without you."

Razor laughed. "Be well, my friend. We will meet again soon." He nodded at me and left.

21

KATHERINE

When I saw Connor put his tongue in that vile creature's mouth, I thought I'd vomit. Words couldn't describe the combination of rage and despair that shot through me. For a moment, all I could do was stare, my fingers twitching involuntarily at my sides. *Dear God, what kind of game is he playing with me?* Here I thought he hated the woman. And I'd let her touch me. My skin crawled at the thought.

As she'd gazed at me with her smug he's-all-mine expression, something spoke to me from somewhere deep within. I would not look like a fool in front of Connor and his paramour. The fact I'd held on to my pride brought me some comfort as pain ripped through me. I'd pushed my shoulders back, stared directly at him while he let her put her hands all over him, and mouthed, "Your loss."

Asha had come running into the restaurant as I walked out. One look at my face, and she'd silently led me to the car. She put the car in gear and drove off, presumably toward the airport. For a moment, every fiber in me rebelled against taking anything touched by Connor. Then logic prevailed— one jet was as good as another no matter the owner.

I stared unseeing out the window, trying to make sense of what had just happened. But I couldn't get past the agonizing pain at Connor's betrayal. If he was that fucking weak willed, I was better off without him. My thoughts spun round and round.

We didn't say a word for the forty minutes it took to get to the airport. Asha pulled up to the hangar of the private air service Connor used.

"I'm so sorry, Kat. Truly. But it isn't what it looks like."

"And what does him having his hands all over her and his tongue down her throat look like, Asha? Never mind the part where he told me they're back together. I'm such a goddamned idiot."

"He loves you, Kat. He just has some commitment issues to work out."

"Yeah, well, if that's what love looks like, I don't want any part of it."

The flight crew were most solicitous, and we'd taken off without incident. The lump in my throat made it difficult to breathe, but I was determined not to cry. I'd cried enough tears over Connor. I wouldn't waste one more drop in his honor.

Eventually, staring out into the dense cloud cover grew old. Thoughts of Connor and our time together threatened to consume me. Connor at the condo in Toronto. *The feel of his hot fingers between my legs.* Connor smiling on the beach at the villa. *His breath hot on the back of my neck as his hands explored my naked body.* Connor laughing as he regaled me with one of his stories. *The heat in his eyes when he wanted me.* Connor at the Masquerade Club. *The feel of his hand as it hit my ass.* Connor caring for me after the accident.

Stop it!

I dug in my carry-on for something, anything to take my mind off Connor. My hand hit the edge of a book, and I pulled it out. Oh shit, the Double Diary.

My first inclination was to throw it or maybe even burn it, but that just wasn't like me. I was a keeper of all things, good and bad. As raw as the hurt was right now, I knew it would fade in time, and I'd be glad for the memories of this magnificent man. *The only man I'll ever love.* This man who was made for me. *Who betrayed me.* I squeezed my eyes tightly shut to hold back the tears that threatened. When I had a grip, I opened the journal at the bookmark.

Double Diary
Connor on September 17 @ 2:35 p.m.

Please believe me when I say that I know you don't understand this sudden change in me. The last thing I want to do is hurt you. I can only hope that when the time is right, you will let me explain. I know you probably don't believe me, but you mean more to me than life itself, and I'm begging you to trust me and give me a little time to work this out. ~C.

Bastard! How dare he? And then the tears came. I sobbed until every muscle hurt and I was gasping for breath. A flight attendant touched my back and asked me whether I was okay. I couldn't respond, not even with gratitude when she handed me a box of tissues.

When every tear had been wrung out of me, I reclined the chair and tried to think. What the hell was I going to do now? I had no job. I'd lost my best friend and now my lover. There was nothing waiting for me in Toronto but a cold, empty house full of memories I'd rather not have at the moment.

I leafed through the diary, and words jumped out at me: I love you. Intimately yours. For more than forever. I slammed it shut and tried to erase thoughts of Connor from my mind. Finally, I knew what I had to do. I rummaged for a pen and wrote him the last note he'd ever get from me. It seemed a fitting, if depressing, way to end the love affair.

Double Diary
Katherine on September 18 @ 10:15 p.m.

You should have trusted me, Connor. If we don't have trust, we have nothing. I loved you, and you betrayed my trust. There's nothing else to say. Enjoy your life. ~Katherine

By the time we landed at the Sky Service hangar at Toronto's Pearson airport, I'd formulated a plan. Connor's driver, Dennis, was waiting at the hangar and quickly loaded my luggage.

"Where to, ma'am?"

Why Connor's staff stood on such formality, I'd never know.

"Take me to my house, please, Dennis."

I steeled myself to enter its tomb-like stillness. He put my luggage in the vestibule, picked up the mail piled on the floor, and handed it to me. I dropped it on the table and dug in my bag for a tip.

"I can't accept that, ma'am. You know that." He smiled to soften the words. "Is there anything else I can do for you?"

"I'll need a ride to the office at some point. Is there a number where I can reach you?"

He reached in his pocket and pulled out a card. "Call any time of the day or night. I'm at your service."

"Thank you, Dennis. I appreciate that."

He left without another word, and I turned to face my memories. I climbed the stairs to Tim's bedroom and stood in the doorway, watching the dust motes dance in the shaft of sunlight shining through the window. An aching sadness at the loss of my dear friend overshadowed the soul-ripping agony of Connor's betrayal. Something about being near what had been Tim's brought me comfort. I lay on his bed, wrapped myself in the comforter, and fell asleep.

I spent the next day checking on the status of my business affairs. Connor, *the bastard,* had assured me that all was taken care of, and he'd been as good as his word. There was only one thing of consequence in the mail, a note from Tim's lawyer asking me to contact her about my inheritance. Bless his heart, even in death, Tim took care of me.

Resolve filled me . . . I had to get out of Dodge. I phoned my travel agent, Charles, and asked him to arrange for a trip to somewhere exotic, like Costa Rica. I really didn't care where as long as the flight left within the next couple of days, and it was far away from any place I'd been with Connor. Charles agreed to courier the ticket and a bunch of tour brochures to me by early evening.

After I returned from Tim's lawyers, I spent the rest of the day packing and planning to be away for a few months. Tim had made me the sole beneficiary of his estate and the substantial insurance policy the university had on his life. He'd left me more than enough to live very comfortably, and more importantly, independently, for the rest of my life. I poured a glass of wine and toasted his memory. *I should have loved* you, *my friend.*

I called Dennis the following morning and had him drop

me at Magnum. As he pulled my rather large suitcase from the car, he asked, "Are you sure I can't drop you somewhere else when you're done, ma'am?"

"No thanks, Dennis. I'll take it from here."

I left the suitcase and carry-on at reception and took the elevator to Connor's office. Stella was once again at the helm.

"Hello, Katherine. It's good to see you again."

"You as well, Stella. I just dropped by to leave this for Connor." I handed her the large manila envelope holding the Double Diary. "Would you give this to him next time you see him, please? No rush."

"Are you sure you wouldn't rather give it to him yourself. He's on his way back right now."

So soon. My treacherous heart said yes, but that road only led to more pain.

"No thanks. But you could call me a taxi. I'm on my way to the airport, Terminal One."

She gave me a look but did as I asked. When she hung up, I offered her my hand. She came around the desk and gave me a hug. I almost started crying again.

"You take care of yourself, dear," she said and patted my shoulder.

As the taxi navigated through the noon-hour traffic, I opened the envelope Charles had sent over and smiled. He'd found me a resort in Costa Rica, and by the look of the brochures he'd sent along, it would be a splendid place to grieve and start anew.

After waiting in a long line of tired and grumpy travelers, I checked my bag and made my way to the security check. I was just about to step through when I heard my name. There was Connor, running toward me and waving frantically.

"Kat, wait. Please."

I turned around and stepped through. My heart beat so fast I thought it would leap out of my chest. Every part of me strained to turn around and go back to him, but my rational brain reminded me it was too late. He'd broken my trust one too many times, and there was no going back. *Jesus, he's been lying since I first met him. He lied about Cecile. He lied about being married. He lied—*

"Ma'am, your purse?"

"Oh sorry, what?"

"We need to scan your purse." I put the purse in the bin on the conveyor belt. The security guard patted my pockets.

I passed through the scanner without incident and waited for my carry-on and purse to arrive on the other side. I picked them up and trundled off toward my gate.

I sat on edge, waiting for Connor to appear, trying to convince myself he had no idea where I was going. A sense of relief and sadness washed over me when the boarding call came. *You really wanted him to find you. No, I didn't. Yes, you did. Oh, shut up.*

I boarded and made my way past the first-class pods to my seat. Now that I was independently wealthy, I'd decided to splurge on a seat in business class.

The pilot gave his welcome announcement and told us to prepare for takeoff. An announcement telling us there'd be a slight delay followed shortly thereafter. *Connor.* I pushed the thought aside. Things like that only happen in the movies.

I buckled in and closed my eyes to discourage any conversation from my seatmate. This time, I couldn't even enjoy my favorite part of flying—taxiing and liftoff. My heart sank as we ascended in the air. He hadn't come for me.

The flight crew demonstrated the emergency procedures, and then the seat belt sign clicked off as we settled at flying altitude.

"Sir, you can't go in there. Please return to your seat."

"Look, it's urgent I see my friend in there. I have something she left behind. It will only take a minute."

My heart leaped into my throat as I imagined the twinkle in those magnetic gray-green eyes and the smile that could melt any heart as he schmoozed the flight attendant into bending the rules. *He came after me!*

"All right, make it quick."

Shit. My palms went damp, and my pulse positively hammered in my ears.

"Kat, there you are." My powder keg of intensity crouched down beside me. "I was afraid I wouldn't find you."

I looked up into that magnificent face, and joy flashed through me. Then I reminded myself that he'd betrayed me. That he was the scum of the earth. I knew I was being dramatic, but it was the only thing keeping me from flinging myself into his arms. I'd made up my mind, and there was no going back.

I gave him my darkest frown. "How did you get here, Connor?"

"It took some doing, but I will not let anything stand in the way of our love ever again."

"We have no love. I see you have the Double Diary. I think my note said it all, Connor."

"Look, Kat. Oh hell." Connor looked at the man sitting beside me. "Do you mind if I take your seat for a moment?"

My seatmate looked at me. "Do you want to talk to him?"

"No, I don't. We've said all there is to say."

"She doesn't want to talk to you," my seatmate said.

Oh great, now *I meet someone gallant.*

"Here, have my seat in first class with five hundred for your trouble." Connor thrust his ticket and the cash at him. The man snatched both and scurried away without a moment's hesitation. Connor sat and reached for my hand. I pulled it away.

"What part of 'you betrayed my trust for the last time' don't you understand?"

"Just hear me out."

If I did that, I'd melt. Not happening. "No, you hear me out. You don't trust me, and you're not willing to commit. Good sex just isn't enough. And what happened to your bimbo, anyway? You couldn't get enough of her a few days ago."

Connor grimaced. "I'm sorry I hurt you, Kat, but I'd do it again. Cecile threatened your life, and I couldn't take the chance that she'd make good on that threat. After all, she'd almost killed you the first time around."

A chill washed through me as the blood drained from my head, and I leaned back against the headrest. "What are you talking about?"

"Cecile and her partner, Ken, are the ones responsible for your accident, and she threatened to kill you or worse if I didn't go along with her plans. She wanted my wealth and power and convinced herself in that misguided mind of hers that you took it all away from her. But she's slippery and covered her tracks, so it took us some time to figure out who was behind the scheme. Then, Brian and I had to be sure we got the proof to put them away for good this time." Connor wrapped a warm hand around mine and squeezed. "Look, can we talk about all of that later?"

"There is no later. Don't you get it? I can't keep living like this." I was determined not to let him suck me in again.

"Kat—"

"No, Connor. Now go back to your seat and leave me alone." I offered him my back as a wall of silence.

"Marry me."

My head swiveled back to him so fast I almost suffered whiplash. "What did you say?"

"Marry me." He pulled a box from his pocket. "I've had this for a while and have just been waiting for the right moment to give it to you."

I peered at the box but didn't touch it. It was too large to be a ring. I narrowed my eyes.

"That doesn't look like a ring box." What game was he playing now?

"It's even better than a ring." He opened the box, and I stared down at an exquisite collar made with knots of yellow gold twisted around a band of filigreed platinum. I held my breath. *Oh, my God.* If there was one thing he could give me to show he was ready to give me his heart, this was that very thing. Anyone who believes the mind holds the greatest power over how we live our lives is wrong. Love and connection are what matters. The longing for both with this man filled my chest and became overwhelming. I choked back the tears streaming down my face.

"I—"

"No more, Kat. I'm here to stay. Until death rips us apart. You are the other half that makes me whole. I can't live another minute without you. I'm not perfect, but I do love you, and I'll spend every last breath earning back your trust. Just say yes."

"Yes."

Joy was the only way to describe his expression as I said the word, but all he said was, "Good. Then set the date." As those sweet lips met mine, my heart sang for joy. Applause and cheers broke out all around us, but the only voice I heard was that of Etta James singing, "At last . . ."

Thank you for reading *Tame Me*! I hope you love Connor and Kat as much, if not more, than I do.

If you're up for one of my sizzling paranormal reverse harem series, check out the Sexy Sins Afterlife Retreat.

Chapter One
Tate

"Am I dead?"

Those are the first words out of my mouth after I land flat on my ass in a throne room. At least, I think it's a throne room. One minute, I was hovering above my comatose body, hoping the angel of death would actually look like Joe Black —yes I have a Brad Pitt fetish. The next, I was plucked out of the room and deposited here. Still dressed in my haute couture hospital gown, I might add. *sigh* Yeah, that's exactly how I want to be dressed when I make my appearance at the pearly gates. Wait—pain and nausea grip my middle. *So,* not *the pearly gates.* My head swims, and I keep it bowed while I take inventory.

I pinch my arm . . . *Ouch.* Okay, I have corporeal presence. Visions of the tornado in *The Wizard of Oz* drift through my mind. *Not the pearly gates. Not Kansas. Oz is also highly unlikely.* Then where the hell am I? I turn in a circle and find my bearings in the iridescent eyes of a stunning woman sitting on an ornate chair. Her flowing gown shimmers as she raises her arm. A second later, a blanket wraps around my shoulders. I tug it across my front, suddenly aware that I'm freezing. At least I'm not in hell . . . I doubt they have manners there.

"No child, you are not dead. You've been chosen for a special mission. We don't have much time before the transition sickness takes hold. Please listen carefully. My name is Hera, and I'm Queen of the Olympian gods."

"Where am I?" I don't care who she is, and this nausea is making me more than a little salty. If she thinks I'm going to sit here quietly and just take whatever she's dishing out, she's got another thought coming.

I open my mouth to speak . . . and can't. The mouth opens, but not a sound comes out. What the fuck? I glare up at Hera. She graces me with a guess-who's-in-charge smile.

"You are in Bardo."

I give her the stink eye. I studied the classics in university, and I know that, as queen of the gods, she has few redeeming qualities.

She looks down at me and smiles. "Don't believe everything you hear. I'm sure I have many good traits."

Name two.

"You'd do well to watch that mouth of yours. I've killed for less."

So, she reads minds. Great.

"Bardo is the realm between realms. Welcome. This will be quick because we have very little time before the ascension cold fever takes over. Right now, your earthly body lies in a coma, allowing you to do the work we need. You will take over as director at one of our schools for one of your Earth months."

Delight battles pain as I realize what she's saying. If this is the afterlife, I can find out what happened to my husband, Bob. Find out if our love was so pure that he's gone on to another life. My heart hammers with fear and hope. *Maybe, just maybe.* My teeth chatter so hard I'm scared they'll chip, but I manage to stammer out the words.

"Is my husband here?"

"Yes. He's here doing the work he needs to do."

My heart does a happy dance, dampened by this damned sickness that's overtaking me. "I need to see him."

"Child, I'm going to speak in your vernacular. Refuse to do this work for us, and we'll pop your ass right back in your body where you can wait another fifty years to see your beloved Bob. Or, do the work you're chosen for and spend the rest of eternity with him."

Well, that was clear.

At least I know how to run a college. But you can't solve organizational problems in a month. Definitely not. Nothing much gets done in the first ninety days if any manager worth her salt is doing the job properly.

"And if this examination center of yours isn't in order in a month?" I so want to give her the stink eye again, but she's just so damned intimidating. Everything about her screams, "Don't fuck with me." It's insane that Zeus was able to fuck around on her and live to tell the tale.

Hera showers me with a triumphant smile. "I have every confidence that with the examiners' help, you'll set things right at the Sexy Sins Retreat."

And speaking of all things weird, who on earth picked such a cheesy name? I mean, really. Of course, then again I'm talking about an entity that marries her brother who, in turn, cheats on her—

The pain ratchets up a notch.

"You'd do wise to park that attitude of yours up here."

More mind reading. Awesome.

"I don't need to read minds when looking at a face as expressive as yours. The name was my idea, and I certainly hope one of the lessons you'll learn is to be far less judgmental."

By now, the pain and nausea are so bad I can barely breathe. *I. Am. Not. Judgmental.*

"Ah, the ascension cold fever has set in. You'll need that taken care of. Once you're over the transition symptoms, the examiners will orient you to your role. Good luck, child." Hera stands and disappears in a flash of light. I lie huddled in a muddled mass of misery.

Wait. But . . . but all I can do is hold my head as a severe headache hits and intense cold racks my body. Then, I'm in the air and snuggled against a large, warm body. *Heat.*

I look up and catch a glimpse of brunette curls framing the most beautiful and familiar face. My mind searches for a thought it can't find—only pain and the need to get rid of it exists. Hera's voice, real or imagined, echoes in my brain.

"One last piece of advice, child, things here are not always what they appear to be. Follow your heart, and all will become clear."

End of Sample
To continue reading, be sure to pick up *Tate's Angel* at your favorite retailer.

ALSO BY LILITH DARVILLE

Wicked Angels Series

Dark Urban Fantasy Romance

Interconnected Standalones

Follow a team of fallen angels as they fight against human trafficking and navigate the blurred lines between good and evil. Set in Pandemonium, a notorious club where they blend in with humans, this heart-pounding series will leave you breathless. Don't miss out on this intense and spicy journey of redemption and second chances.

.

Rogue Angels Series

Dark Urban Fantasy Romance

Completed Series

Rogue Angels is a twist retelling of the Snow White fairytale. Enjoy an adventure with fated mates, midlife crisis, and evil demons. This story includes themes of love, sacrifice, and self-discovery.

.

Sexy Sins Afterlife Retreat Series

Paranormal Reverse Harem Romance

Completed Series

Warning: This series has one strong woman and four dangerously sexy immortal men. She's been their fated mate in every life they've lived and they refuse to live one without her. Read this series if you like why choose romance with a paranormal twist and hunky guys times four!

.

Masquerade Club Series

Dark Contemporary Romance

Completed Series

A contemporary saga with a side dish of spice and a second chance romance for two people you'll never forget. The Masquerade Club is exclusive and available only for the ultra-rich where all your dreams and fantasies come true. Join the party and fall in love with Connor and Katherine in this angst-ridden suspense-filled series.

.

ABOUT THE AUTHOR

Lilith Darville is a *USA Today* bestselling author of dangerously delicious romance, including sizzling paranormal reverse harem. With over forty years of storytelling experience, her stories are guaranteed to make readers flush and blush.

lilithdarville.com

ACKNOWLEDGMENTS

I remain grateful for the hard work of my editor, Maggie Morris, and her hard work, commitment and enthusiasm. I appreciate her for her efforts in making this an even stronger story. Continued huge thanks go to my cover artist, Melanie Card. She's been incredibly talented and the consummate professional.

I salute my researcher, Michael O'Brien, for the many hours he spent helping me 'navigate' through the streets of Miramar, Cannes, and Nice. I beg his forgiveness for the moments when I grew testy—yes, I know, hard to believe—while we struggled with computer glitches. A huge shout-out to the amazing Jenny Bartlett for coming up with the title fraud scheme. Of course, I would be remiss if I didn't recognize the contributions of my beta readers, especially the inimitable Tracy Reitzel.

To my readers and fans, a hearty thanks and keep those comments and suggestions coming.

Words are powerless to express my gratitude for my biggest fan and supporter, my husband, Bob, for his indulgence, encouragement, and collaboration. It's been quite a ride, and one I hope continues for many, many years to come.

www.ingramcontent.com/pod-product-compliance
Lightning Source LLC
Chambersburg PA
CBHW061348310726
48974CB00001B/243